FUMBLED

a novel

HARRY BRADY

Fumbled
Harry Brady

ISBN (Print Edition): 978-1-54398-672-3
ISBN (eBook Edition): 978-1-54398-673-0

To Shirley, Becky and Teresa

CHAPTER

1

Forbes Field Pittsburgh, PA - December 9, 1949, 3:54 P.M.

It was freezing, literally freezing, sitting in the stands at Forbes Field that Sunday afternoon watching the Pittsburgh Steelers and Philadelphia Eagles battle it out for the league lead.

The thirty-eight degrees at kickoff had dropped to the bone chilling thirty-one with a much lower wind chill factor. All of the remaining ninety five-hundred or so stalwart paying fans, and a little over one hundred freebees in the bleachers, seemed to shiver in unison uncertain that they were shivering due to the cold or due to the dire situation on the field of play. The KDKA radio broadcast was blaring over the public address system, "Two minutes and twenty seconds left in the game and the Eagles have the ball first and goal on the Steelers five yard line with Pittsburgh hanging on to a thirteen to ten lead. Hansen takes the snap hands off to Cunningham off left tackle. He breaks through to the three, WOW!! What a hit! The ball is out!! The Steelers have it!" As hearty a cheer that the freezing fans can muster filled the stadium.

"Two players are down, Cunningham and number eighty-eight for the Steelers, the rookie linebacker Skrcyzinski. The trainers are out and Skrcyzinski is up, but appears a little groggy. Cunningham has not moved and the team doctor is running onto the field. This does not look good." On the field, the doctor and team trainer for the Eagles checked the still motionless player. After a few minutes, the doctor signaled for a stretcher. When it arrived he carefully immobilized Cunningham`s head and neck as the downed player was put on the stretcher. An ambulance came out of the runway in right field, as the stretcher was moved to the sidelines and then into the rear of the ambulance. Number eighty-eight, Damien Skrcyzinski, stood silently by and watched as the trainer and doctor both entered the rear of the ambulance still attending to the injured Philadelphia running back. The rear door was closed and after the ambulance left the field he walked unsteadily back to the Steelers bench.

Steelers Locker Room - 4:15 P.M. that afternoon

The smell of sweat, beer, testosterone, and boisterous shouting provided the setting for Abe Fletcher and his KDKA radio crew to conduct the postgame interviews. "Congratulations Damien Skrcyzinski you forced the fumble and saved the game for the Steelers. Describe the play for us."

"All I remember was the full back coming into my territory and I hated him. I put my head down and aimed at his helmet."

"Did you see the ball come out?"

"No! The next thing I remembered was sitting here in the locker room with a ferocious headache and people patting me on the back and everyone celebrating because we won."

"Well you took a big hit out there yourself, but in essence you won the game and the Steelers now lead the division. The Chicago Bears are next on the schedule. Maybe you can give the Bears a headache next week."

"Don`t worry about me. I`ve had my bell rung numerous times over the years and I`ll be at Soldier`s Field in Chicago ready to play next Sunday."

Zone One Pittsburgh Police headquarters
Homicide Division - December 4, 2018

Damien Skrcyzinski sat quietly in the interrogation room at Zone One headquarters on Pittsburgh`s north side. He stared blankly at the beige walls of the stuffy twelve by fourteen room. He put his elbows on the metal table and rested his head in his hands. He was somewhat confused but that is not unusual for him these days. How did this happen he asked himself.

"I`m a football player not a murderer. I don`t know what they are talking about. Why am I here?" Detective Phillip Cash from homicide entered the room and walked over to the metal table where Damien Skrcyzinski sat with his head in his hands. Pulling out a metal chair directly across from Damien he sat down. "O.K., Mr. Skrcyzinski, we've been at this for two hours now. Let`s try again. You understand this is a murder investigation and we just want to know your whereabouts on Friday evening September twenty eighth and also Thursday evening November fifteenth. Another thing, we need to know is where did you get the drugs that were in your room?"

Looking up Damien Skrcyzinski answered, "I told you I don`t remember where I was any day in September or November fifteenth and the drugs weren`t mine."

"Is that all you have to say?"

"My brain doesn`t work the way it used to. The doctors said it was from all the head trauma from playing football. I just don`t remember things."

"I get that part. We`ve read you your rights. Do you want a lawyer?"

"No! I want to talk to Millie."

"Who`s Millie?" Detective Cash asked.

"She`s my friend at Holy Angels Retirement Community. You can call her there."

After the detective left the room, Damien put his elbows back on the table and rested his head in his oversized hands. "I just can`t remember what happened a few days ago. I don`t even remember what I had for dinner last night," he said out loud to the walls. Then, he mentally began to take stock of what his long-term memory could bring back.

His first memory was when he was in the second grade and he found out that his father had been killed in the war.

His memory then jumped to when he was on a football field playing against the University of Indiana. It was a cold and rainy day and the field was muddy. It was a very physical game and not much scoring. All afternoon he had been bumping heads with Indiana`s All American tight end, Chuck Jacoby. Jacoby was all he could handle, and there had been more than one helmet to helmet collision. His memory then jumped to the College All Star game that year in Chicago, when he and Chuck Jacoby were All Star teammates. They had a few laughs over which one of them had the hardest head.

His memory was freewheeling now, he pictured in his mind when he tackled Johnny Lujack for a safety against Notre Dame. That was the only score for his team in that game, as they got steamrolled by the Fighting Irish. If I can remember that, why can`t I remember recent events he anguished to himself.

His next flash back was about Maria his high school sweetheart. He met her in the school cafeteria one afternoon while she was holding court with several members of the football team. He had noticed her many times previously, but he was too shy to start a conversation with her. In his mind she was the most gorgeous woman he had ever seen. A dark haired full bodied Italian beauty, who was very popular with everyone at the school. He had walked over to the group and started talking to one of his friends who introduced him to Maria. Her first words to him were, "Don`t you play football for the Trojans?" From that moment on there was no other girl for him. They married the week after he graduated from college. Damien smiled inwardly at this warm fuzzy memory. Then this inward happiness was invaded by that tragic day, when Maria and their five-year old daughter were involved in a fatal crash on an icy highway near Wexford Pennsylvania. At that point he felt that his life was over. His football days had ended and he became a loner, drinking heavily. As painful as these memories were Damien tried to jog his failing memory for more details. What came into his mind at this point was the sad story of the heavy drinking and the bad investments "friends" had advised him about. The next step was sleeping in a homeless shelter and spending his time panhandling on the Pittsburgh streets. He tried to recall how he got out of the homeless shelter and into Holy Angels Retirement Community. All of these details were not sharp, but he remembered that the National Football League had said that it wasn`t their fault for his memory problems and they did not owe him anything. Someone had told him to get a lawyer to sue the league but he did not have any money for that. He remembered standing outside the Steeler's stadium one Sunday before one of their home games when one of his former teammates from the nineteen forties saw him and started a conversation. This is when the memory became foggy again. However, he did remember that about a week later the former team mate contacted Damien with the news that "Once a Steeler always a Steeler" and funds for his moving in and living at Holy Angels Retirement Community were being taken care of by an anonymous individual.

CHAPTER

2

New Iberia, LA - August 22, 2018

The call came in at six forty-five that morning to the 911 operator. An early morning jogger had found the body of a young woman in some bushes along the banks of the Bayou Teche. Detective Bill Malone had been notified at home, and by the time he arrived at the scene a patrol car was there with its flashing red and blue lights leading him to the exact spot where a young woman`s life had ended.

It was already hot and humid as Malone got out of his car. This day will be a scorcher, he thought as he walked toward the banks. The fog had begun to clear over the Bayou Teche, and he observed a blue heron indignantly flutter its wings and fly off while casting a glance at him as if to say, "How dare you disturb my breakfast in this serene setting."

As he moved a few yards further, things were not so serene as he came upon the body of the young woman halfway down an embankment. The New Iberia patrolman was standing next to the body and recognized the detective. "Nothing has been touched and the coroner is on his way. I also notified the lab people to come and do their stuff."

"What does it look like to you?" Malone asked.

"No obvious signs of trauma. It looks like she either fell or got pushed down the embankment."

Malone eased himself down the slope to get a better view of the scene. "First off, she wasn`t jogging with those red stiletto heels."

The woman`s body was on her back with arms and legs akimbo. She was African American and appeared to be in her early twenties. The expression on her face was placid. She was wearing a short sleeved, bright red sheath dress and had ruby red lipstick. Her eyes were open and the color dark brown. They were staring up at the morning sky as if she was looking for a blue heron. Malone bent down and looking at the left arm could see the needle tracks of a mainline drug user. Looking around the area no needles or syringes were found and no purse or wallet. As he walked back up the embankment, he wiped a few beads of perspiration from his forehead, got in his car, put the air conditioner on high, and headed back over the drawbridge toward the New Iberia court house, which also was the site of police headquarters.

Deputy Sheriff Carrie Landry was in her office when Detective Bill Malone arrived back at headquarters. Knocking lightly on her door and entering simultaneously, he walked up to her desk. Carrie looked up from some paperwork she was studying and said, "Thanks for waiting for me to say 'Come in' and thanks for tracking mud over the department's new carpeting."

"You should know by now, I'm not house broken."

"Okay Bill, what did you find over on the bayou?"

"Young African American female. No Identification. A main line user. Possible overdose. No signs of a struggle. I think the body may have been dumped there because you can drive right up to the area."

"Where do we go with this one? What`s your next step?"

"We need a time of death and a full toxicology drug panel. I think she`s probably a hooker. I`ll pick up a picture from the crime scene people and show it around."

"So you think she overdosed, and whoever was with her panicked and dumped her body in the bayou."

"That could be the narrative, but do you remember about a month ago the body of a prostitute they found in the Bayou up in St. Martinville. No trauma, fully clothed. The toxicology there showed a fentanyl overdose. The similarities are there. In addition to that, I talked to a sheriff`s deputy over in Morgan City last week. He told me about a new batch of fentanyl that`s come into the area. It`s apparently coming up through Florida from Central America. From what he said, this new stuff is ten times more potent than heroin and when the druggies try to switch from heroin, some of them end up dead."

"Interesting info, Bill. Stay on this case and let me know what the toxicology shows." With that Carrie Landry looked back at her mound of paperwork and Malone turned and walked out of her office tracking more Louisiana mud on the new departmental carpeting.

CHAPTER

3

The 3 to 11 shift was leaving the New Iberia Medical Center on East Main. Raymond Benson stepped out of the air conditioning into the still, hot, and humid night. By the time he got to his 1950 Ford pickup, a few beads of perspiration formed on his forehead. He glanced over and saw the fog already forming over the Bayou Teche. Looking to the sky he saw a few flashes of lightning and knew a storm was rolling in. Getting in the rusty and dusty truck, a few large raindrops splattered on the wind shield forming miniature mud puddles. Starting the engine, he put the truck in gear and slowly exited the parking lot onto East Main, as the rain increased. He stopped at the 24 hour convenience store on the corner of Bridge Street and picked up a six pack of Dixie beer.

This was Raymond`s favorite brand, even though it was presently being brewed in Wisconsin. Dixie was first brewed in nineteen hundred and seven and was a staple of the Cajun beer drinkers until the brewery was destroyed by hurricane Katrina. The Wisconsin Dixie beer wasn`t as good as the old Louisiana Dixie beer, but it was cheap enough for his budget. Crossing the drawbridge over Bayou Teche, he entered the City Park and stopped at one of the pavilions. He got out and entering the pavilion popped the top of a beer. He took a big first swallow and sat on one of the benches to wait for the two teenagers, who wanted to buy some weed from him. It was his last bag, but he needed some cash and he could steal a couple of baggies from his grandmother's stash later that evening.

The rain had abated somewhat and promptly at 11:30 two teen age girls walked into the back of the pavilion and approached Raymond's bench. The taller one's blond hair was wet and stringy and the other girl was shorter and heavier and she had on a Ragin Cajun dark baseball cap. The shorter one asked, "Are you Raymond?"

He responded "Yeah, do you have the cash?"

She reached into her jeans pocket and silently pulled out several crumpled bills and handed them to him. He counted the money and told her to follow him back to his truck. When they got there he reached under the front seat and produced a baggie containing the marijuana and handed it to her.

Getting in on the driver's side Raymond smiled and said to the blond girl, "I've got some beer and I know where we can go and have some fun together. How about it?"

"Not with you, Loser Boy!" she laughed and pulling on the sleeve of her friend, they turned and ran laughing back into the pavilion and out the back entrance.

Raymond yelled, "That's the last weed you'll ever get from me you little whores." He closed his door and thought to himself, if those little whores ever call me again for any weed, they may end up like those other ones in the bayou. He finished his Dixie beer and started the engine. Looking at the exit road, it began again. At first it was as if a searchlight was flashing straight ahead and getting larger and larger. Then it was the lightning bolts blue, red, and yellow across his vision but Raymond knew that they were not real. What he did know was a horrendous throbbing headache was coming and it would last all night. It was those damn little whores that caused it, and he swore that he would get even with them the next time. He turned off the engine and rested his head on the steering wheel and closed his eyes.

The searchlight was gone, but the red, blue, and yellow lightning flashes remained. After about fifteen to twenty minutes later, the visual aura faded and a throbbing headache began on the right side. He restarted the engine and eased out of the city park and turned onto the road to St. Martinville. As he traveled the rain slick two lane blacktop, he began brooding to himself as he considered all women to be bitches and tonight he would get even with that smart mouthed deputy sheriff up in St. Martinville. She was the one that got his driver's license suspended for a third DUI. He knew where she lived and he would get his revenge this night.

Arriving on Main Street in St. Martinville, a small town that was a throwback to the 1930s, he drove slowly past the Evangeline Oak and St. Martin`s church. When he came to the deputy`s street, he turned left and turned off the head lights. He knew she was working the night shift and when he passed her house he saw that there was no car in the driveway. He parked half a block away and getting out of the truck reached in and took a half gallon jug of ammonia out of the back of the pickup. Looking at the neat white frame house, he saw his targets. On either side of the front steps leading up to the gallery were two large azalea bushes in full bloom. On the gallery deck were three hanging baskets flowing over with multicolored flowers. Opening the jug he dealt with the azaleas first and then the hanging baskets. He quickly finished his work and putting the cap back on the jug smiled to himself, that this would get even with that smart mouthed bitch. He threw the empty jug into the back of his truck and set out for home, his headache pounding and getting worse.

About five miles north of St. Martinville, Raymond turned off onto a gravel road that led to the Bayou Teche. On the corner was Boudreau`s Grocery and Live Bait Store run by his grandmother and her live-in boyfriend, Aldous Hebert. Aldous was a former worker on the gas pipeline and allegedly had enough back problems, that he was retired on disability. Despite being on disability, Aldous was known as a mean drunk and someone to be avoided in all the local saloons.

Raymond pulled into the gravel lot and parked around the back of the store and entered through the back door and into the living quarters.

"Where the hell you been?" roared Aldous. "You need some explainin' to do." He was sitting on a greasy, old easy chair with a small table next to it. On the table was an almost empty bottle of Jim Beam. A black and white cowboy movie blared on the television. Raymond`s grandmother, Jewel Boudreau, was lying on an overstuffed couch across the room sound asleep. At the sound of Aldous` voice, she sat up in a daze.

Stepping into the center of the room Raymond replied, "I ain`t done nothin' wrong."

"The hell you ain't!" Aldous yelled at him and got up and gave him a hard backhand across his face.

"You been stealin` meth and baggies of weed outta Jewel`s stash for weeks."

"I ain't stole nothin'!" Raymond wailed as he felt a trickle of blood running down his upper lip.

Fully alert now, Jewel joined in, " Yes, he has Aldous. Several baggies was missin' last week and two this morning. He also took a bunch of meth pills last week. You gotta teach him a good lesson this time."

"I ain't gonna take it no more. I ain't gonna take it no more." Raymond kept saying to himself.

"Wipe the blood off your face, you snot nosed son of a bitch! Get your ass into the back storeroom and I`m gonna teach you a lesson you ain't never gonna forget. I gotta piss first, and then it`s comin." Raymond ran from the living room back through a hallway toward the storage room. He grabbed the 44 gauge shotgun from the corner of the store room and slammed the door. By this time Raymond felt like his head was exploding. "I ain`t gonna take it no more. Everybody hates me! My mother hated me! She left me in a bait store, so she could go and be a whore in New Orleans. I got no friends. Aldous and Granny hate me! I just ain't gonna take it!"

Just then, Aldous Hebert kicked the door open and zipped up his fly. The last thing Aldous Hebert saw on this planet was the cold double barrels aimed directly at his face.

"What the hell`s goin` on back there" Jewel Boudreaux yelled as she ran down the hall toward the storeroom. She let out a shriek that could wake all the Banshees in the Bayou Teche, as she looked at the blood ,brains, and left eyeball splattered on the floor next to what used to be her live-in boyfriend.

"Don`t worry, Grandma, you`re next." Raymond hissed as he calmly reloaded and aimed the double barrels at her chest and fired. Calmly stepping over the two bodies, Raymond went to his room and packed an old duffel bag with some clothes and went back into the storeroom. He then pushed a packing case out of the way exposing a trap door. Reaching down, he lifted the door he removed all of his grandmother`s stash of drugs, which included marijuana, heroin, meth, and a bag of the new fentanyl. Stepping back over the bodies, he went out and got in his truck and drove out of the gravel driveway and headed north for his new life.

About 9;15 A.M. the next morning, Butt Jenkins and his wife, Georgia, pulled onto the gravel lot at Boudreaux`s Grocery and Live Bait Store. Still high from the meth they had bought from Jewel last night, they wanted to score some heroin from Granny. The front door to the store was still locked from the night before. "They usually open by eight," Butt commented. "Let`s go around back and see if we can wake the old gal up."

He banged on the back door several times with no response, so Buck tried the door knob and found that the door was unlocked. Opening it and stepping inside he hollered, "Anybody home?"

After there was no response he and Georgia stepped in to the living room. The television had an Andy Hardy movie running and Butt noticed the almost empty Jim Beam bottle on the side table. He said to Georgia "They must have a hell of a hangover after all that whiskey." He hollered again, "Anybody home?" and they proceeded down the hallway. When they saw the gory scene, it sobered them up immediately and uncharacteristically they called the police. Butt gave some details of the scene to the dispatcher at sheriff`s office, but declined to give his name. Georgia took one more look at the grisly scene and ran out the back door and vomited on the gravel driveway. Butt followed her out and they got in their pickup truck and left Boudreau`s Grocery and Live Bait Store.

Deputy Sheriff Carrie Landry and Detective Bill Malone arrived 10 minutes later. The back door was open and checking behind the counter they found that the cash drawer in an ancient brass cash register had

Been emptied. Based on the call in, they proceeded down the hall where they found the bloody mess. Stepping over the bodies they looked further into the storeroom and found that two boards had been lifted up and reaching into the space, they found a yellow plastic basket with several baggies, a teaspoon, a butter knife, and a faint trace of white powder.

Carrie spoke first, "I`ll call the lab techs and the coroner, and why don`t you look around and see what you can find."

After checking the inside and outside thoroughly, Bill Malone reported that there was a small amount of blood next to the cash register and the Boudreaux`s old Ford 150 pickup truck was gone from the parking lot. No shotgun was found anywhere.

"They have a teenage grandson that lives with them and his room looks like he didn`t sleep here last night. We need to find him and notify him about his grandparents."

Back at the station, Carrie, all 175 pounds of her, was at her desk finishing a whopper and fries when Bill strolled in. "I pulled the files on the Jewel Boudreaux and her live-in Aldous Hebert. They are a nice family. He has a long rap sheet of disorderly conduct, aggravated assault and resisting arrest. Jewel has several narcotic charges. Apparently in addition to selling groceries and live bait, she also did some drug dealing out the back door. Their daughter, the kid`s mother, was found dead of an overdose in a cat house off Bourbon Street in New Orleans when he was only three years old. I contacted the juvenile court and his records are sealed but what I got from his juvie officer is that he has been in constant trouble with the law."

After taking this all in, as well as finishing the whopper, Carrie asked about any adult charges.

Bill continued, "One time a neighbor filed a complaint that he killed their dog with a shotgun. He claimed that he thought it was a nutria. The damn dog was a Yorkie."

Carrie looked up again and asked "What was his name again?"

"Raymond Boudreau."

"Now I remember him. That's the guy, I pulled his license for a third DUI last week. He had an old beat up truck. It was not at the scene of the shootings. We need to look for it locally and I put out a BOLO on it, as well as a description of this guy."

CHAPTER

4

At 7:05 P.M. that evening, Raymond walked out of the front door of a rest station on an Interstate north of Little Rock. He carried all of his possessions except the shotgun in a large brown duffel bag. They included a change of clothes, several bags of white powder, 3 vials of methamphetamine pills, and a brown bag full of marijuana. There was also a bag of the new fentanyl pills that Granny had recently obtained. The shotgun was stashed under the front seat of his pickup. As he looked over to his parking space, Raymond froze in place. There he saw two Arkansas state troopers looking at the license plates and then checking the doors. Making an abrupt turn he hurried back into the rest station and out the rear door to where the large trucks are parked. He spotted a driver climbing into a large orange semi-tractor. Approaching the semi he yelled, "Where are you heading?"

The driver responded "Where do you want to go?"

"Wherever you are going" Raymond answered.

The driver waved him over. Raymond jumped in and threw his duffel bag up behind the passenger seat and closed the door. The driver eased out to the exit ramp and gaining speed pulled the bright orange rig onto the Interstate. After getting up to speed Raymond asked, "Where are we going?"

"I've got a load of watermelons to drop off in Pennsylvania and they need to be there by morning."

"Ain't never been to Pennsylvania." Raymond responded.

"Truth is ain't never been north of Little Rock. How far is it?"

"We got over seven-hundred miles to go, and I'll do some high ballin' to get us there on time. My name is Carl. What do you go by?"

"Raymond."

"Well sit tight, Raymond, I just took a couple of No-Doz and we're up to eighty-five now and no radar for one-hundred miles."

The hum of the tires and the fatigue of the day lulled Raymond into a fitful sleep. He was abruptly awakened by, "Radar up ahead in Missouri, so I'm cutting her back to seventy-two."

"You running away from something Raymond?"

"I ain't runnin'. Just wanted to get out of Cajun country for a while."

"Can't blame you much for that. Some of them Cajuns are crazy. Ran into a bunch of them in a bar in Breaux Bridge. Tough guys, they about tore the place down. Scared me off Raymond".

"Ain't no Cajuns gonna scare me ever again".

"We're past the radar, so I'll boost her up till we get into Illinois. We can hit Interstate seventy and a straight shot to Pennsylvania"

Once again the hum of the tires and the monotony of the flat-lands lulled Raymond back to sleep He awoke to the strange sensation of a popping in his ears and looked at the mountain looming ahead. "Where in the hell are we?" he asked.

"This is West Virginia and We`re going up Wheeling Mountain. Pittsburgh isn`t far. What do you plan to do when we get there?"

"Haven`t decided yet."

"What kind of work do you do?"

Raymond hesitated for a second and thought to himself "My last job and only real job." Then he answered, "I was working in a hospital."

"If you need some cash, when I drop off my load on produce row you can pick up a few bucks unloading the truck. After that I can drop you off downtown. I`ve got a girlfriend there and she`ll put me up for the night."

"I guess downtown will be OK . I`ll find someplace to sleep. Maybe the bus station."

"Hey, why don`t I check with my gal and see if she has a friend available for you? It would be a hell of a lot better than sleeping on a bench in the bus station, and you`ll have a few bucks from the produce yard. You could get a motel for the night."

The load of watermelons rolled on into western Pennsylvania and turned north onto interstate seventy- nine through the Liberty Tubes then across the bridge over the Monongahela River and headed east for produce row in the Strip District of Pittsburgh. When they arrived at Carl`s destination, he pulled his rig off the main road and entered a staging area overlooking the Allegheny River. On the driver`s side were railroad tracks where several box cars were being unloaded into smaller local delivery trucks. On the passenger side was a long a long stretch of spaces for the tractor trailers to back up to the unloading platforms. Carl got on his cell phone and made a call. "I got number twenty three," he told Raymond. Carl then slowly drove the semi slowly to about the midpoint of the line of docks and then backed the big rig into a dock with a big twenty-three above the space and turned off the engine. "See that guy with the Pirate baseball cap standing by the office door? He hires the day labor. His name is Larry. Tell him I sent you over, and he`ll get you on. I`m going to climb up in the sack and get some sleep, while I wait for them to get to my truck."

Raymond got out went over to Larry and soon was assigned to space number two unloading corn from central Illinois.

5

Since Carl was a freelance trucker, he owned his own tractor and once the trailer was unloaded, he pulled his tractor to a parking area. Carl waited for Raymond to collect his day wages. Once Raymond was paid in cash, he went over to the parking area and looked for the bright orange tractor. Climbing up on the driver's side, he rapped on the window to awaken his new friend. Carl rolled over in the sleeper compartment and pressed his remote to open the passenger door. Raymond hopped down and crossing in front of the rig climbed up and got in on that side. Carl greeted him with, "Let`s go have some fun." Starting the engine the orange tractor pulled out onto Liberty Avenue and headed for the Thirty-First Street Bridge. Crossing the Allegheny River to the Northside they turned west and headed for Federal Street.

Federal Street was on the lower Northside of Pittsburgh and was an older part of the city that had been settled by German immigrants back in the 1850s. Traveling along the main drag through this part of town Raymond was amazed by solid red brick buildings that had been built over one hundred years ago. Many of them were boarded up and some had been vandalized. Zingers Bar was at the corner of Federal and Isabella streets. Back in the 1930s, Federal Street was a vibrant

Northside commercial center, but urban decay started early here and was progressive to the present day. Despite being renamed, the North Shore Zone during redevelopment attempts, this area still had one of the highest crime rates in the city. Now it consisted mainly of pawn shops, saloons, betting parlors and a cheap motel that had a blue neon sign in the window advertising "Day Rates."

Carl parked half a block down Isabella Street and they walked to the corner. Zingers Bar had a greasy front window that held a sign advertising cold beer and hot sandwiches along with a green neon sign for Iron City Beer. Carl and Raymond entered the front door. The interior of the bar was no more inviting then the exterior. It smelled of sour beer and burnt grease. On the walls were pictures of former Pittsburgh Pirates and Steelers. The bar itself looked like it was a time warp from the1930s. A huge mirror on the wall behind the bar extolled the virtues of Old Guckenheimer the bar liquor, a blended whiskey for two dollars and fifty cents a shot. At the far end of the bar was a moderately pudgy woman sitting on a bar stool wearing a bright red dress, that exposed two equally pudgy knees. Her hair was a reddish maroon, a color that Raymond had never seen in New Iberia. Waving to them she got up and came over to give Carl a major league kiss. Coming up for air Carl simply said," Laverne this is Raymond". Laverne extended her hand and said to Raymond, "You boys have got to be thirsty after that long drive. Let`s get a booth and get something to drink." Raymond did not reach out to touch her hand but mumbled, "We could use a beer."

After they had chosen a booth, a waitress came over to take the bar order. Carl ordered three Iron Citys. The waitress came back promptly with the beer and proceeded to take the food order. Carl wanted a cheeseburger and fries, as did Raymond. Laverne opted for the Double Header Special, which consisted of two burgers with bacon, cheese and two sides.

"My friend, Sandi, said she would love to meet you Raymond. She should be here in about 15 minutes. You`ll like her she is full of fun."

Just as the food arrived so did a very thin female in a similar bright red dress with matching lipstick and a pound of mascara. Her hair was jet black and her eyes betrayed many years of hard living. As the waitress put the food in front of them, Laverne said, "Sandi, why don`t you order something to eat and sit down so you and Raymond can get acquainted." Sandi responded that she was not hungry and ordered a vodka on the rocks. Sliding into the booth next to Raymond, she put her hand on his thigh and said, "Tell me about your trip." Raymond`s left thigh twitched but he didn`t answer. He looked at the Old Guckenheimer sign behind the bar and saw a searchlight coming toward him. He knew what was coming next. The red, blue, and yellow lightning flashes in the mirror.

Laverne looked at him and asked the same question, "What about your trip?"

He responded "I think I`m getting a headache."

CHAPTER

**Ballroom at Holy Angels Retirement Community
- November 26, 2018, 8:55 P.M.**

Damien Skrcyzinski and Millie Estel were standing aside at the exit door from the ballroom at Holy Angels Retirement Community, as the motorized scooters and walker assisted residents file out of the auditorium. Then they fell in line behind with the remaining cane users and the more agile residents.

"Damien, what did you think of the quartet and the vocalist that did the Perry Como tribute?"

"I always liked barbershop quartets and Perry Como was always one of my favorites. I met him one time when I was still with the Steelers."

"Which one of his songs did you like best?"

"I can`t remember the names of the songs, but I do know he was one of my favorites".

They arrived at the elevator and saw the mass of canes, scooters, and walkers waiting there and decided to take the stairs. Upon arriving at the third level, Damien huffing and puffing opened the door and let Millie go first into the hallway.

"Rita was discharged today from Allegheny General Hospital and is in the nursing unit for a day or two. Damien let`s go by and say goodnight before we turn in."

"What was the reason she was in the hospital?"

"As I told you yesterday at breakfast, she has a heart condition. When she went to her cardiologist he did an electrocardiogram and said something about her heart rhythm and admitted her to the hospital for some tests. He changed her medicine and wants her to be monitored here."

Walking down the hall past their apartments, they arrived at the heavy wooden doors leading into the nursing unit. Once again Damien held the door open for Millie to enter. They proceeded past rooms 365 through 355 on the right until they reached the nurses station. The lights were dimmed and sitting at a desk staring at his cell phone was a man in blue scrubs.

"Excuse me sir, can you tell me what room Rita Bailey is in?" Millie asked.

Without looking up from his phone he said, "Visiting hours are over it`s after nine o`clock."

"We live here we will just look in and say goodnight to our friend."

This time looking up from his phone he said, "Lady, I told you visiting hours are over for today. Try again tomorrow."

Damien and Millie turned and started walking back toward the residents' hallway. Halfway there Damien said to Millie "I saw her file in the chart rack. She is in room 365 we can look in on our way back to our apartments."

Walking back down the hall Damien asked Millie if she knew the man at the nurses' desk. Millie said, "He has been here for a few months and his name is Raymond. He is the night orderly and he never is very friendly. Stopping at room 365 Damien started to open the door to let Millie enter. Just then Raymond came running down the hallway and got in front of Millie pushed her back from the entry way.

"I told you no visitors and that means no visitors" he snarled at her.

At this point Damien grabbed Raymond by his shirt and pinned him against the wall and said, "Where are your manners? If you ever touch that lady again I`ll break you in two! Millie, why don`t you go in and say goodnight to Rita for both of us".

Millie entered the room and a few seconds later she came out screaming "Damien, It`s Rita. She`s not breathing!"

Releasing his grip on the shirt he let Raymond slip down the wall to the floor.

Rushing into room 365 Damien saw a motionless Rita curled up in a ball. She was not breathing and her lips and fingernails were turning blue.

Damien had seen this situation before on the streets of the lower Northside and immediately recognized an opioid overdose. "We need Narcan and we need it NOW!" he said to a frightened Millie.

Rushing out the door he grabbed Raymond again by the shirt and dragged him to the nurses' station.

Pulling Raymond`s shirt until they were inches apart he said, "Get the key to the narcotic cabinet and open it now"

Raymond snarled back "I ain't got no key and the head nurse ain't here."

Tightening his grip Damien demanded "Where is she?"

"She`s over in the memory unit and won`t be back for twenty minutes."

At this point Damien flung Raymond against the counter with a corresponding crack of several ribs.

Grabbing the door of the medicine cabinet Damien used all his strength and fury to tear the door from its hinges and reached in and grabbed the antidote. Running back to room 365 he burst in where Rita still laid motionless. Millie was at the bedside slapping Rita`s hand and calling her name loudly in a vain in an attempt to revive her. Millie stepped aside and Damien rolled up Rita`s sleeve and took the preloaded syringe and setting the needle and syringe in place injected the Narcan into Rita`s left triceps muscle. He then joined Millie who had begun reciting the Hail Mary.

A few minutes later Rita`s eyes fluttered and she rolled over on her back and asked, "What are you and Damien doing here? It`s after visiting hours."

CHAPTER

7

It looks like a quiet night, Jeannie Edwards thought to herself as she left the memory care unit. All the meds had been given and the only problem was Mrs. Ellis looking in the linen closet for her cat, Gizmo. All that took was assuring Mrs. Ellis that Gizmo would show up in the morning and giving her an Ambien to help her get to sleep. Silently moving down the hallway she relaxed as she thought of her cappuccino waiting back at the nursing station on Three South. Being the night supervisor in a retirement community was a much less stressful job than the 18 years she had spent as an emergency room nurse at Mercy Hospital in downtown Pittsburgh. No more gunshot wounds, stabbings, drunks, overdoses, or other unsavory things that were a nightly occurrence. She didn`t have to deal with the chaos of multiple severe injuries from automobile accidents on the highways. Then she relived her emotional strain when she recalled the night four college boys were brought into the emergency room after the car they had been riding in was hit head on by a tractor trailer traveling at high speed on a two way black top. Two of the boys were so badly injured that they were dead on arrival. A third boy was barely breathing and despite the heroic efforts of the emergency team he died within the hour. Jeannie was there when the parents arrived to receive the awful news. In her mind she knew that it would a night she would never be able to forget. The fourth boy miraculously survived with multiple orthopedic injuries. Coming back to the present she thought the only stress here at Holy Angels had been those three sudden deaths during the last two months. There had been no autopsies, so the official cause of death was recorded as cardiac failure even though there was no solid evidence to support that diagnosis. As a matter of fact the doctor who signed the death certificate was covering for the house doctor and had never actually seen the patients. Well, we are getting into the holiday season she thought so all is calm and all is bright and all I want is my coffee tonight. Opening the heavy wooden door to the skilled nursing unit her first sight was that of Raymond slumped against the counter in the nursing station. He was holding both arms against his chest and appeared to be in a great deal of pain. "Raymond, what in the world are you doing there!"

"It`s not my fault!! It`s him that giant. He hurt me!! Then he stole the medicine. I ain't gonna take it!!

"Raymond slow down. What giant and what medicine?"

"It`s that football player and that know it all woman he pals around with. They stole the narcotics!"

Wincing in pain Raymond braced himself against the counter with his right arm tried to stand up. Yowling in pain he yelled at Jeannie, "That son of a bitch broke my ribs. I ain't gonna take it."

Jeannie turned to look at the narcotics cabinet and gasped in disbelief. Vials of drugs and syringes were scattered about the cabinet and several bottles had fallen on the floor. She tried to process what she was dealing with when the door to room 365 opened and Millie stepped out and walked up to the nurses station.

A confused Jeannie asked, "Millie, do you have any idea of what's going on?"

"Rita overdosed on a narcotic and Damien saved her," was Millie's calm reply.

Getting right in Millie's face Raymond screamed, "That's bullshit!! That's bullshit!! He stole the narcotics and broke my ribs."

Just then Damien stepped through the door of room 365 and saw Raymond threatening Millie again. He grabbed Raymond by his scrub shirt and slammed against the opposite wall. Wailing in pain Raymond crumpled to the floor and curled into the fetal position.

Millie stepped in front of Damien, who was now bending over the crumpled Raymond. "Damien stop!!!" She ordered. "Why don't you go wait in your apartment. I'll be right there."

"What about him?" Damien asked pointing to Raymond.

"In his condition, he isn't going to hurt anyone. Now please go to your room."

Damien looked at Millie with the expression of a twelve year old who had just broken the family heirloom vase and obediently left for his apartment.

Jeannie had thought that she had seen just about everything from her emergency room experiences, but this was getting out of hand. Her first instinct was always her patient's wellbeing. Rushing into the room, she saw the bedside table pushed to the side and a spilled water pitcher on the floor. Going over to the bed she looked at the patient who appeared to be perfectly comfortable and asked "Mrs. Bailey, are you O.K.?"

Rita Bailey now alert and lucid said, "I feel fine. What is all the commotion about in the hallway?"

Checking her pulse Jeanie said, "I`ll tell you about it later." Satisfied with a strong pulse, Jeannie put a blood pressure cuff on Rita`s left arm and felt comfortable with a 137/75 reading. Jeannie handed Rita the call button and told her, "I`ll check back with you in a little while. If you need anything, just push the button. "

Turning to Millie, who had followed her into the room she said, "Let`s go to the nurses station. I need to call security while you tell me what is going on." After they left the room Jeannie called security and said they had an emergency and needed someone right away.

Raymond was getting into a sitting position, as they arrived back at the nurses' station. Going over to him, Jeannie helped him stand and said, "Come with me to the exam room and let me check you out. From what you said we may need to get a chest x-ray." As Jeannie helped Raymond to the exam room she glanced back at the dismembered narcotic cabinet. "And I thought this was going to be a quiet night." she said to Millie.

Millie reassured her with, "I will explain everything after you deal with security and check Raymond out."

After evaluating Raymond`s injuries, Jeannie was satisfied that he was stable. She returned to the nurses' station, where she and Millie waited for security to arrive. During this time, Millie gave Jeannie a narrative of the incident.

After about twenty minutes, the security guard arrived with an apology that the lady in apartment 220 had accidentally pulled the panic cord in her bathroom and he was responding to that when he got the call to the health center.

Jeannie politely accepted the apology and asked him to call a cab for Raymond and send him to Mercy Hospital for chest x-rays. When security had left, Jeannie explained to Millie that she would have to do an inventory of the drug cabinet to determine what had been stolen and she needed to secure the remaining drugs. She then asked Millie to stay at the nurses' station while she checked in on Rita first. When she returned to the nurses' station satisfied with her patient's wellbeing Millie asked her if she could be of any help. Jeannie responded, "I've got some coffee brewing. Let's take five, and then you can help me check what's left in the drug cabinet." The inventory disclosed that the only missing drug was the Narcan, and the empty syringe that had been recovered from Rita's room. The next step was to place all the drugs back in the cabinet, tape the door back on, and sealing it as best they could with duct tape until the morning. After Millie left, Jeannie sat down to write an incident report and thought maybe emergency room duty wasn't so bad after all.

CHAPTER

Emergency Room Mercy Hospital - November 26-27, 2018

While sitting in the examining room waiting for the cab to arrive to take him to Mercy Hospital, Raymond could feel it starting again. The searchlight coming at him then the red, blue, and yellow lightning bolts started whether he had his eyes open or closed. By the time the cab arrived at the emergency room entrance, his head was throbbing and he felt like vomiting. He got out of the cab and handed the driver the voucher the security guard had provided him. Wincing from the pain, he entered through the sliding doors and walked up to the reception desk. A young man asked if he could help him, and Raymond said that some SOB had just broken his ribs and the nurse at Holy Angels sent him to the hospital to get an x-ray. The young man handed Raymond a clip board and a pen and asked him to fill out a medical history form. He directed him to take a seat in the waiting area. Raymond walked into the room and looked around. In one corner was a woman with a small child wrapped in a pink knitted blanket that she was gently rocking the child back and forth. In another corner, he saw a man his head back against a wall and apparently asleep. In the center of the room stood a circular table which was covered with old magazines and several half emptied Styrofoam cups. Raymond decided on a chair as far away from the other people as he could. He eased himself down while cursing at the pain under his breath. After a few minutes, the woman with the baby was called in by an attendant. The questionnaire was three pages long and the first line asked for his full name. Raymond put down his new name that he had assumed since leaving Louisiana, *Raymond Benson.*

The forms asked several questions that he did not understand. When he got to the part on family medical history, he almost laughed at the question of whether or not his mother or grandmother had a history of diabetes. Then his anger welled up again as he thought, what difference did it make because his mother was a whore and she died from a drug overdose and Granny had been blown away by his double gauge shotgun. His bile grew worse with the next question about his father's medical history. Hell! He never knew who that bastard was!!

At this point, he threw the pen on the table and answered no more of the damn questions. After another short wait, Raymond was called in by the same attendant he had seen previously and taken to another room where he gave his Holy Angels insurance card. After all the pertinent information had been recorded he was escorted through a hallway past several examining cubicles some of which had curtains drawn. Doctors and nurses were scurrying in and out of the cubicles. A uniformed police officer was apparently standing guard by another cubicle. Crying, cursing and prayers were the sounds he heard as he was led back to an examining room. It took about five hours until Raymond walked out of the hospital and got in the cab to take him to his place of residence. On the ride there, he grumbled to himself about how it took five hours to tell him that he had broken ribs. He told them that when he first got there. Then, they said there wasn't anything to do, but let it heal on its own over four to six weeks. However, the best part was they gave him a prescription for OxyContin. He was to take it three times a day for six weeks. That`s 126 pills he read on the prescription form. Then he thought I`m gonna make me some money out of this.

When he arrived back at the rooming house on Lockhart Street where he was living, he went up to his "apartment" as the owner of the property called it. Going up to the second floor he went into his apartment and collapsed on a moldy overstuffed sofa. After a minute or two, he slouched back further into the overstuffed sofa and his fog began to clear and his senses sharpened. Even with the OxyContin from the emergency room visit, his ribs still hurt like hell. Putting his head into one of the pillows he was almost overwhelmed by the smell of vomit, urine and sweat that reeked from it. His mind was racing. I ain't gonna take it from that big ape. He`s gonna go down! I ain't gonna take it any more from nobody.

As the fog continued to clear he realized that he hadn`t eaten since yesterday afternoon. Pushing himself up wincing and cursing he went to the kitchen counter where he looked for something to eat. Seeing some Taco Bell bags, he looked for any leftovers and all he accomplished was to disturb several roaches that scurried off to the safety behind some empty beer cans.

Falling back onto the couch he began to plot his revenge. One more of those old whiny bitches from the home are gonna go, and Mr. Skrzz, whatever the hell his name, is will go with them. He opened the bottle of OxyContin took one out even though he wasn`t due for one for another four hours and swallowed it with the next to last swig of Seagrams left on the table. He closed his eyes and went into a fitful sleep. When he awoke it, was daylight out and he had to use the toilet. He got up and opened the apartment door and walked down the hall to the communal bathroom. The door was locked. It was in use. He banged on the door and growled "Hurry up. I gotta go real bad."

"O.K. O.K. give me a minute!" came a female voice.

Raymond danced up and down the hall for a few moments until he heard the lock open and a middle aged woman in curlers and a wearing a dirty yellow bathrobe exited and giving him a dirty look she turned and walked away down the hall without saying a word. Feeling relieved after using the facility he returned to his room. He finished the last of the Seagrams on the table put on his jacket and headed out to Taco Bell.

CHAPTER

9

The Executive Director`s Office - The Next Morning

It was a bright cold December morning with a few scattered snow-flakes falling as Detective LaKeisha Johnson from the narcotics unit pulled into the parking lot at Holy Angels Retirement Community. She had never been there before and was impressed how neat the grounds looked even in winter. There were two buildings each of which was three stories of the red brick construction, so common in the Pittsburgh area. She pulled the black Ford Crown Victoria into one of the visitors' parking spaces and got out. Walking toward the front entrance she observed two life size concrete Holy Angels standing guard on either side of the front entrance. Upon entering she asked a cheerful elderly lady at the reception desk for directions to the Executive Director`s office. As directed, she walked down the hallway to the right. Looking for office 110, she noticed some workers were taking turkeys and pilgrims cutouts off the office doors and were replacing them with Rudolphs and Santas. She thought that may be rushing the season, but it may help cheer up some of the lonely residents. Nearing the end of the hallway she reached a door that read Marilynn Cassidy,

MPH, Executive Director. Underneath this were the words, Please Come In. Detective Johnson knocked gently and opened the door.

Upon entering, she was greeted by a trim middle aged woman with slightly graying blond hair put up in a neat bun. She was dressed in a navy blue business suit and white blouse. On the suit jacket was a name tag that read, Marilyn.

Marilyn Cassidy turned off her computer and stepped from behind her desk extended her hand and said, "Welcome to Holy Angels, Detective Johnson. Thank you for coming to our community."

Taking her hand Detective Johnson responded, "It sounds like Holy Angels had an exciting time last night. Since there was a question of a drug overdose and narcotic cabinet broken into, it fell into my area. Maybe you can clear up some of the confusion."

Turning toward an attractive mature woman in a nurses uniform, she introduced Jeannie Edwards to the detective. "Our night nursing supervisor in the care center, Mrs. Edwards, has agreed to stay to talk with you, Detective Johnson. Would either of you like some coffee?"

"No, thank you." LaKeisha Johnson responded. Jeannie Edwards said, "I`m all caffeined up from last night and don`t need any more, Marilyn."

"O.K. Let`s sit down and sort things out," Marilyn said as she gestured toward two chairs in front of her desk.

"Detective Johnson, where would you like to start?"

"Last night, the desk sergeant got a phone call about midnight from one of your employees. The employee was in the E.R. at Mercy Hospital with some broken ribs. He was ranting about one of your residents, a giant, who had assaulted him and broken into the narcotic cabinet. He was also ranting about some fentanyl. The desk sergeant said he was somewhat confused and advised him to come to the station and file a written report. The man declined to come in and began cursing and slammed the phone down. So when Holy Angels called to report the situation, I felt it best to get the facts correctly from you."

"Jeannie, you were there why don't you tell us what happened," Marilyn suggested.

Jeannie began by saying it was a quiet night and when she returned from making rounds in the memory unit she found a chaotic scene in the skilled nursing unit.

After about a ten-minute description of the night's events by the Jeannie Edwards, LaKeisha sat back and responded. "Let me get this straight. We have a giant with some memory problems going into the nursing unit after hours and deciding one of the patients is having an opioid overdose, and he tears the door off the narcotic cabinet and steals nothing but Narcan. He then assaults one of your employees and proceeds to inject the designated patient with Narcan. This is when you arrived on the scene Mrs. Edwards and when you checked the patient she seemed perfectly fine."

"Yes, Detective, that's about it, except we don't have any fentanyl in our formulary."

"Mrs. Edwards why would a nursing home have Narcan on hand? None of the patients would have access to fentanyl or heroin would they?"

"We do stock Narcan for some emergencies, like cardiogenic shock or septic shock. Fortunately we have never had occasion to use it."

"Please tell me about the assailant. The man who called it in called him a giant and a wild man."

Jeannie continued "Well he is a very big man and apparently very strong. He was a professional football player and Raymond Benson , our night orderly, did have several broken ribs."

"What about the "the wild man" description?"

Jeannie continued. "The assailant is known here as a gentle person, but he did seem very aggressive last night."

"What about his memory problems?"

"He does have some memory problems, but then again there are times he does function quite well."

Turning to the Executive Director, Detective Johnson said, "I will need the name of the assailant. We may need to talk to him later.

Then turning to Jeannie Edwards she said, "Mrs. Edwards, thank you for the information and thank you for staying to talk with me. At first glance, it looks like we have a simple assault case and not a narcotic theft. If you would kindly provide me with Mr. Benson`s contact information, we will contact him and see if he wants to file a formal charge against the resident."

"Thank you Detective Johnson, Holy Angels will conduct our own internal security investigation. Pending what our investigation determines, it looks like we may need to consider taking action regarding Mr. Skrcyzinski`s behavior and if there is the need for him to be in the secure memory unit."

Detective LaKeisha Johnson walked out past the two life-size concrete Holy Angels guarding the front entrance of Holy Angels. She got in the Crown Victoria and started the engine. Before putting it in gear, she thought for a moment as to how someone with a memory problem would have the knowledge to diagnose a drug overdose and then how to reverse it with Narcan. She also wondered why the man with the broken ribs was sure that it was a fentanyl overdose. With these unresolved questions in her mind she put the car in gear and drove back to the Zone One Police headquarters.

CHAPTER
10

Zone 1 District Squad Room

Later that morning, Detective Johnson walked into the Zone 1 district squad room and approached her four feet by five feet cubicle and laid down the notes she had taken over at Holy Angels. Sitting at the next cubicle was detective Phillip Cash who looked up from his computer and asked, "What`s up, LaKeisha?".

"Nothing much. Just got back from Holy Angels with a bizarre story that ended up as a simple assault. How about homicide?"

"Slow night last night. I just got the tox report back on the hooker who was found dead in the Day and Night Motel on Federal Street. No foul play. Over dosed on fentanyl rather than heroin. There`s a new batch of fentanyl that`s come in about a week ago and it is super potent. It seems as though the addicts try to switch from heroin to the new stuff and it`s taking them out."

"What else do you have on that case?"

"I talked to the desk clerk and he told me that she had come in that afternoon with a scraggly looking guy carrying a large duffel bag. He left about forty-five minutes later with the duffel bag. They didn`t discover the body until the next morning until the cleaning lady found her. She was fully clothed and no signs of any trauma."

LaKeisha walked over to the coffee machine and asked, "Want me to warm up your cup?"

"No thanks, I`m fine. How`s Tyrone doing? I understand he made the varsity as a sophomore."

"That boy! He keeps growing. Six feet two inches and he`s only fifteen. He got to start their last game and scored twelve points. How about Robin?"

"She got her report card yesterday and it was all AAAs."

LaKeisha settled into her chair, set the coffee down and picked up the phone to call a Mr. Raymond Benson to see if he wanted to file an assault charge against a Mr. Damien Skrcyzinski.

The cell phone lying under the cocktail table in the rooming house at 518 Lockhart Street rang seven times before a mumbled hello answered.

"This is detective Johnson with the Zone One Police Department. I`d like to speak to Raymond Benson."

"Yeah"

"Is this Mr. Benson?"

"Yeah, whadda ya want?"

"You called in last night about an assault at Holy Angels. You know the assailant and where he lives. Do you want to come down to the station and file a formal complaint?"

Still in a fog from the previous night's hydrocodone and Seagrams Raymond slumped down on the couch and tried to think.

"So that's the bastards name. Forget it! No, no charges. I can deal with it myself." Before LaKeisha could respond the call was disconnected.

It looks like there may be more excitement at Holy Angels detective LaKeisha Johnson thought to herself.

"Hey Cash, what's up with the cupcakes over by the coffee machine?" He looked up from a report he was writing on his computer and responded, "It's Sargent O'Connor's birthday and he brought them in to celebrate, because he has only two more years before he can retire. Does your victim want to file charges?"

"No, he isn't going to press charges and the more that I think about this it may not be just a simple assault. " LaKeisha then related the questions she had in her mind after leaving the meeting at the Executive Director's office at Holy Angels.

"As soon as I finish one of those cupcakes, I'll go down and wish Sargent O'Connor a happy birthday. Then I think I will pay a visit to the two combatants."

"Why don't I tag along? I don't see how a 95 year old lady in a nursing home would try to get high on some fentanyl. Somebody may have wanted her to die."

CHAPTER
11

About fifteen minutes later in an unmarked car, they drove down North Avenue turned right onto Cedar leading to the lower Northside and then a few blocks later a left onto Lockhart Street. It was a very narrow street with large rambling houses that would have been fashionable in the 1920s era, but were now either boarded up or had "rooms for rent" signs in cracked front windows. It was a scene typical of many large cities across the country. Arriving at the address Marilyn Cassidy had given to LaKeisha, they parked and entered a red brick building through an unlocked front door into a short hallway with steps on the right going up to the second floor. On the second floor landing they found another hall with several doors each of which was numbered. Proceeding to #216, Cash knocked on the door. After a few seconds with no response he knocked again. A muffled, "Yeah," answered, and then, "Whatta ya want?"

Cash responded "Police, we just want to ask you some questions."

The door opened just enough for Raymond to look out and for Cash to flash his badge.

The door opened further allowing them to enter the room.

Raymond stepped back pulling up and buttoning his jeans saying "I ain`t done nothing wrong."

La Keisha took the lead at this point "We didn`t say you did, we just want to ask you about the incident at Holy Angels and the resident that allegedly assaulted you."

Raymond stepped across the room and flopped back on the greasy couch said, "That big son of a bitch broke my ribs. That`s what happened."

Both Cash and LaKeisha looked for a place to sit down but seeing the roaches and Taco Bell bags scattered all over the room, they decided to remain standing. "What led up to that?" La Keisha asked.

"I don`t remember. All I know is he broke my ribs and it still hurts like hell."

"What about the lady who you gave a pill to?"

"I never gave no lady any pills."

"She said you did."

"I ain`t allowed to give out pills. Them old people is so looney over there, they don`t even know what day it is."

Further questioning only resulted in more complaints about broken ribs and that he would get even with that big SOB.

Retreating from the roach motel, Cash and LaKeisha got back in the car. "What`s next?" Cash asked.

"While we are in the area, let`s stop at the Shamrock Café and see if our giant is there". Five minutes later they pulled up in front of the Shamrock Café. Walking in, they looked back along the booths on the right. Four card players were in the last booth and intent on their game. Sitting on a chair next to the booth was a huge man watching the proceedings.

Approaching the group, all activity stopped and Cash and LaKeisha became the center of attention. Facing the huge man from the side LaKeisha asked him, "Are you Damien Skrcyzinski?"

Standing up and towering over her, Damien said, "Yes, I am. What can I help you with?"

Flashing her badge LaKeisha answered, "We`d like to ask you some questions?"

"That`s okay with me. I always enjoy talking about football."

"No, it`s not football. It`s about an incident at Holy Angels. Let`s go to another booth where we can talk."

Walking back to the first booth where they were out of earshot from the card players and two patrons at the end of bar, they all slid into the booth with Damien on one side facing the two detectives. La Keisha began, "Tell us what happened the night, you thought the lady was having an overdose."

"My friend and I were going to visit another friend in the nursing unit and when we got there, I saw that she had overdosed and I gave her Narcan and she got better."

"Why did you think she had overdosed?"

"I didn`t think it. I saw it."

"O.K. how did you know it?"

"If you hang around this neighborhood all the time, you can see one of those every couple of days."

"O.K. How did you know it was fentanyl?"

"They all look the same. Heroin, cocaine, fentanyl - they all look dead and turn blue."

"O.K. but why did you know it was fentanyl?"

"The talk on the street is that fentanyl is the newest drug in town."

Just then an older man walked in and waved to Damien. "I see you have some new friends. Have you shown them your picture next to Bullet Bill Dudley?" Both LaKeisha and Cash thought to themselves, "Who is Bullet Bill Dudley?"

Further questioning over the next ten minutes was not productive, so they returned to the unmarked car and got in.

"Now what do we do?" asked LaKeisha.

"How about we do lunch at Max and Irma`s. Get you some good German food. Seven minutes later they walked into Max and Irma`s Hof Brau Haus. The décor suggested that you were in a hunting lodge somewhere in the Black Forest. A large stag`s head was mounted above the bar and beer steins lined the counter of the back bar. An elderly lady with her gray hair up in a bun came up and took Cash`s hand said in an accent, "Phillip, where have you been? You and your lovely wife Laura should come here more often. I still remember when you used to come here every day when you were a little boy to deliver our newspaper."

Smiling at her he said, "Yes, and Max would always give me a free glass of coke. It`s been at least twenty- five years since I delivered the papers. Irma, I want you to meet my friend Detective Johnson. She needs some good German food."

"Well, you brought her to the right place. We have sauerbraten, potato pancakes and red cabbage as a special today. Can I get you something to drink before I go back into the kitchen?"

"Black coffee for both of us," Cash replied.

When they were seated in a back room LaKeisha asked, "What do you think about this morning?"

"From what you said, the nurse has the best info. She has every-thing documented and the Executive Director was scared. No confused is a better term. As for the orderly, when I looked at his eyes I saw only anger and cold hatred. I also think that he did not give up a Rhodes scholarship to work as an orderly at Holy Angels. The football player seems to be street wise and knows drugs and how to use Narcan. We also need to find out who the hell Bullet Bill Dudley is."

LaKeisha laughed. Their food arrived and they dug in.

CHAPTER

12

As the snow began to fall "Slick Johnny" Anderson stepped out of the front door of the Shamrock Café on East General Robinson Street and began walking toward Federal Street a block and a half away. He was more than a little pissed that one of his regular customers had failed to show up. Even though it was overcast and snowing, he put on his sunglasses because he felt that it added to his street credibility. This was his territory and he needed to remind everyone the he was THE MAN on the lower Northside. His kingdom ran from the Allegheny River on the south up through Fineview to Perrysville Avenue to the north. The eastern edge was all the way up Troy Hill and to the west it went out Brighton Road almost to the Western Penitentiary, where many of his friends resided. If anyone tried to move drugs in his domain he had a former middleweight boxer as his muscle. A few broken jawbones and kneecaps secured his empire.

John Jefferson Anderson considered himself a very smart man even though he had dropped out of school in the sixth grade. He was the youngest of eight children in a single parent home. His mother was on welfare, but there was never enough money. As a result he never remembered having any new article of clothing for himself, even his underwear. All he got to wear were hand me downs from his older brothers and in the sixth grade the only warm coat he had came from an older sister. He remembered the kids in his classroom making fun of him and calling him a girl. That was one of the reasons he stopped going to school. At age eleven he became the lookout for a local drug pusher on River Avenue. It didn`t take long for him to buy a Pittsburgh Pirates jacket at the local Sears and Roebucks. The next step was to become a runner for the dealer delivering baggies of marijuana and various other illegal substances all over the Northside. This allowed him to gain a knowledge of all the streets in this part of the city and who were the best customers for these various products. By the age of fourteen, he had his own daily route similar to a newspaper boy. This enabled him to become one of the flashiest teen age dressers in town and to move out of the rat infested flea bag, that he had grown up in.

The next major move in his career path was to lie to the police in defense of a local hood, who was accused of breaking into a jewelry store on East Ohio Street. Johnny arranged to hide the stolen property before the police could get a warrant to search the suspect`s apartment and then provided an alibi by telling the police that the hood was in an all-night poker game at the time of the robbery. Then came Johnny`s earning his name of "Slick Johnny." Johnny took the stolen jewelry and sold it to a fence, who was on Johnny`s regular drug delivery route. Johnny was sure that the hood would not retaliate because it was known that Johnny had the protection of the drug dealer`s enforcer.

Then at the age of twenty two, good fortune smiled upon Slick Johnny once again. Johnny`s boss, the main man in the Northside illegal drug trafficking business, got himself shot and killed in a big stakes crap game in Steubenville, Ohio. Because of his intimate knowledge of the territory and customer needs, Slick Johnny by default took control of the Northside drug business. He inherited the burnt out second rate boxer as the businesses muscle. Slick Johnny solidified his position by offering a better deal to his wholesale drug suppliers, and then deftly raised the price of the drugs to his customers. This made Slick Johnny richer than his wildest dreams. He now had a chauffeur to drive him around in a pink Cadillac. He had sexy women, and he could buy all the new clothes he ever wanted. He was certainly The Man on the Northside of Pittsburgh.

Halfway down the block on the opposite side of the street was a black Cadillac Escalade with darkened windows. The rear window opened and a voice called out, "Hey, Slick Johnny."

As Johnny looked over at the Cadillac, he saw the business end of an Ak-47 poking out of the window and the flash of a short burst. Johnny was thrown back against a wall and slid down onto the sidewalk as rivers of bright red blood ran down his camel hair overcoat. The front door of the Cadillac opened and a short man with a dark complexion ran across the street and going through Slick Johnny's overcoat pocket found his cell phone and put it in his own pocket and then hurried back to the car.

So on this snowy morning as the Cadillac slowly pulled away, Slick Johnny Anderson was no longer The Man ruling the drug traffic on Pittsburgh's lower Northside.

Fifteen minutes later Detectives Phillip Cash and LaKeisha Johnson arrived on the scene. Yellow tape was already up preserving the crime scene. Since it was an obvious homicide, Cash from homicide took the lead and approached a patrolman trying to disperse the small crowd that had gathered.

Flashing his badge he introduced himself and said, "I'm Cash from homicide. What do we know so far?" The patrolman shooed a couple of teenagers away and turning to Cash said, "The victim is someone known as Slick Johnny. Apparently he was blown away by someone in a dark sports utility vehicle."

Detective Lakeisha Johnson tapped Cash on the shoulder, "I know Slick Johnny from narcotics. He`s a local dealer with a long rap sheet for narcotics and pimping. He uses local muscle to control things. No fireworks."

Turning back to the patrolman Cash asked, "Any witnesses?"

"There are about half a dozen witnesses in the Shamrock Café two doors down. That`s where he was coming from when he got hit. My partner is holding them there for you guys."

Cash stepped under the yellow tape and turned toward Johnson. "Let me check the scene out here and you can get out of the snow and start with the witnesses". LaKeisha turned away and walked toward a door with a large green neon shamrock marking the entrance to the cafe.

As Cash went over to the body the snow began to come down harder in large flakes. Slick Johnny`s sunglasses had fallen off and laid next to his right hand. The rivulets of blood on his overcoat had begun to clot and the large snowflakes were giving them the bizarre appearance of little candy canes. Cash went over to the place where the Cadillac Escalade had parked, and to his surprise found a shell casing lying in the gutter. Putting the shell casing in a baggie he completed his evaluation of the crime scene and crossed back over the street and went into the warmth of the Shamrock Café. Looking around, he thought he had entered a time warp from the thirties and forties. The bar was long and its polished mahogany extended almost the entire length of one wall. The back bar had a double shelf that held almost any liquor known to modern civilization. A mirrored wall extended almost the entire length of the bar. On the opposite side of the Shamrock Café were dark brown booths extending back to two doors that appeared to open into a kitchen area. In the last booth were four card players who looked up briefly at Cash and went back to their game. On the dark paneled walls were sports pictures of all Pittsburgh athletes going back to the Pirates' Honus Wagner and up to Ralph Kiner, Bill Mazeroski, and Roberto Clemente. The Steelers Terry Bradshaw and Franco Harris had prominent spots, as did the boxer Fritzi Zivic.

Detective Johnson was over at the front of the bar talking to the bartender. Seeing Cash she offered, "Slick Johnny was to meet someone here. Apparently he came in, didn`t order anything and kept checking his watch. After about 20 minutes, he left." Pointing to the bartender she said, "This is Fred and he said Slick Johnny is not a regular here but sometimes waits outside to meet people.

At this point, Fred interrupted and said, "We don`t allow any drug deals in here. I think he came in today to get out of the snow and cold."

"What about other witnesses?" Cash asked LaKeisha.

She replied, "The same four guys that were playing pinochle the last time we were here claimed that they didn`t see a thing. The big guy standing by the window is the football player that was involved in the assault at Holy Angels. He heard the gunfire and looked out the window in time to see a black sports utility vehicle with dark windows drive by. Fred said he is a regular and comes in almost daily. I`ve got all the names and info if we want to talk to anybody later."

Cash said, "Give me a few minutes with the guy by the window and we can head back".

Cash went over to the window and flashed his badge to Damien and had a brief discussion with him.

Back in the car Cash said, "The big guy was interesting. He`s a former Steeler, who played back in the 1940s. He likes to hang out at the Shamrock Café, because that is where the players would go after a game. The owner Art Rooney would come in buy them beer and burgers. If they won the game it would be steaks. He says his picture is hanging on the wall by the third booth next to that of Bullet Bill Dudley`s".

"Who is this guy named Bullet Bill Dudley?" Johnson asked. Then she continued, "This shooting was a gangland type assassination which makes me think we may have a turf war in the making".

"You mean the brothers on Wylie Ave are moving in on the Northside" Cash asked.

"No, this isn`t black on black. The new guys are Korean."

"What? The only Koreans I know around here own restaurants and cleaners."

"Cash, do I have to educate you on everything?" She then went on to explain to him about the Kkangpae and the South Korean mafia. They got their start back in the mid-1950s in Seoul during the turbulence after the cease fire had been signed with North Korea. Basically they extorted protection money from Korean merchants. Then in the nineteen seventies and eighties, they infiltrated larger businesses and set up connections with some government officials. From there it was the next logical step to global crime rings. That is how it all began in the United States. The particular branch we think are moving into Western Pennsylvania began in Incheon and Suwon have ended up in New York City. Because of their turf wars with the Chinese Green Dragons, they have been looking for places to expand their operations, specifically into the Rust Belt." She continued her story, "Cities like Ambridge, Aliquippa, and Monongahela are small towns and presented no problem for them to muscle in on the small time dealers. These are bad dudes and they deal in extortion, drug and human trafficking. Violence is their primary MO. In Queens, they operate out of a martial arts gym. Now that they are here in Western Pennsylvania, we have some big time problems."

She paused for a moment and then continued, "I referred to them as the Korean mafia. They are not exactly the same as we know the mafia here. There are no families, like in New York mafia, where different families go to war with each other. They function more as a brotherhood, in which an established Khangpae boss will recruit young men they feel have the qualities that would benefit the organization. The older man then takes on the role of an older brother, who mentors the younger man on how to become a loyal Khangpae operative. This is somewhat akin to a mafia soldier becoming a "made man.""

Queens, New York

It was snowing and cold in Pittsburgh that day, but sunny and cold in Queens, New York. Lee Heon Tae was finishing a blueberry bagel at Starbuck`s when his cell phone buzzed. Recognizing the number, Lee answered with the colloquial Korean hello, "Yoboseo".

The voice on the other end said simply in perfect English, "Slick Johnny retired from the sales department this morning".

"Good work, my little brother. What is your next step?"

"We have his cell phone, which has a list of all of his customers. I plan to contact them all today. There should be no problems once we let them know they are now buying from Kkangpae."

Lee said, "Keep up the good work and keep me informed." With that he disconnected and took another bite of his bagel and felt an inward warmth that he had chosen a good man to take into the brotherhood.

CHAPTER
13

The snow was coming down heavily now as Raymond stepped out of
the Taco Bell. Wearing tennis shoes, a grimy light jacket, and no cap
he began to shiver as a wind gust hit him in the face with a wind chill
factor of five degrees. Damn it`s cold here, he thought to himself. It
ain't never this cold in New Iberia. He remembered seeing a Goodwill
store over on Federal Street and headed in that direction to buy some
warm clothes. About ten minutes later, he approached the front door
of the store. Brushing the snow off his jacket and shaking it out of his
more than ever scraggly hair he stepped inside. An overhead vent was
blowing warm air and Raymond stood under it. After he warmed up a
little, he looked around. Seeing a rack of coats and jackets on his right,
he went over and spotted a maroon quilted jacket that didn`t look too
worn. It had a six dollar tag on it. It was a little big but it would keep him
warm. Next he went to a pile of caps, put on a black corduroy Elmer
Fudd style cap with ear flaps priced at one-dollar and fifty-cents, and
went over to the cashier. Pulling out two fives from his pocket he paid
her, received his change, and went back out into the storm and headed
back to his Lockhart Street apartment.

His feet were wet and freezing as he walked up the stairs and opened the door. Going in, he flopped on the moldy couch and took off his wet socks and tennis shoes. He emptied his pockets and came up with a total of seven dollars and sixty- five cents. Walking over to his bed in a small alcove, he raised the mattress and pulled out a Walmart bag that contained his drug money. He knew that he had enough to buy a week's supply of meth for himself and his three customers. He could also buy the heroin for the janitor at Holy Angels and the janitor's girlfriend.

Stuffing the cash into his pocket, he put on his only other pair of socks, his wet tennis shoes and set out for Uncle Sam's Military Salvage store to get some combat boots and heavy wool socks.

Uncle Sam's was one of the few places left where Raymond knew he could buy army surplus combat boots. He arrived at the store and found some heavy wool socks in one of the aisles and going to the shoe department found his size combat boots from a stack of shoe boxes. He paid the cashier and then sat down on a bench near the front door and proceeded to take off his now wet socks and his soaked tennis shoes. He put on his new wool socks and combat boots and placed his wet shoes and socks in the shoe box and placed it in the plastic bag with Uncle Sam's logo on it. He then exited the store. The cashier and another customer who was checking out watched this in silence. After Raymond left, the cashier commented to the customer, "We certainly get all kinds of people in this place."

With his new warm clothes and dry feet, Raymond set out for his meeting with Slick Johnny at the Shamrock Café. He knew he was late but he felt confident that Johnny would give him the drugs and wait until payday for his money. Johnny had done this once before when Raymond first came to town. As he approached East General Robinson Street, the snow began to fall more heavily. Then he noticed two patrol cars on the corner. At the intersection he looked down the block and saw a small crowd, some cops, and yellow crime scene tape. He hesitated on the corner trying to discern what was going on. As he stood there, two teenagers broke away from the crowd and came walking toward him. He stopped them and asked what was causing all the excitement. One of them replied, "Some black dude just got gunned down coming out of the Shamrock." The teenagers continued walking around the corner, and Raymond stood there for a moment and then began to walk cautiously toward the crime scene. When he reached the yellow crime scene tape, he saw the camel hair overcoat and sunglasses and immediately Raymond knew that he had a big problem. He turned his back to walk away and had no feelings for Slick Johnny's demise. Raymond's only concern at this point was how he could get a new supply of drugs for himself and his customers. All he had left was one baggie of weed in his room and the potent fentanyl he had taken from Granny's stash. He had spent a good part of his drug money on his new warm clothes and his rent was due soon. The snow continued to fall heavily as he walked back toward his apartment on Lockhart Street. The only stop on the way was a liquor store where he purchased another pint bottle of Seagrams and a six pack of Iron City beer. The only reason he was drinking Iron City beer was because it was cheap and they didn't sell Dixie beer in Pittsburgh.

Later that afternoon in his apartment as he was getting ready to go to his 3:00 P.M. to 11:00 P.M. shift at Holy Angels, his cell phone rang. Someone named Tom announced that Slick Johnny had retired and Raymond would now be getting his "groceries" from Tom. Everything would be a cash only deal and prices were going up.

Raymond said, "What if I have another dealer?"

"You don't understand the situation. Pay attention," Tom said, "unless you buy from me you may retire permanently along with Slick

Johnny." Raymond hesitantly gave Tom his weekly order and asked when he could get it.

Tom answered, "Same time same place as with Johnny. Remember cash only." And the phone went dead. Raymond went over to the counter by the sink and took a swig from the already opened bottle of Seagrams. He then opened a can of the Iron City beer and took a big swallow as a chaser. Then he put on his quilted jacket followed by his Elmer Fudd hat. He sat down on the overstuffed moldy couch and tied the laces on his combat boots. He got up and chugged the last of the beer and left the apartment for Holy Angels.

Later that afternoon in the health care center, Raymond watched for the 4:20 P.M. exodus from the resident's apartment hall for the four-thirty buffet in the ballroom. He knew everyone would be going, because today's menu would be a Mexican fiesta theme and there would be appropriate music and decorations. Watching through the windows in the heavy brown doors he waited until the parade of canes, walkers, and scooters had gone down on the elevator. Entering the resident hallway he surreptitiously checked each apartment until he found an unlocked door. Opening it he entered into a small living room and glanced around. He saw that it had some football pictures on the wall and a crucifix. There was a cocktail table with a Sports Illustrated magazine on it and some other magazines scattered on a couch and on the floor. Against the opposite wall was a small television set. Going into the bedroom he saw that the bed was unmade and shirts, under wear and socks were scattered over the bed and on a dresser. Next was a small room apparently functioned as a den. On a desk was a picture of an attractive woman with a young girl blowing out candles on a birthday cake. Above the desk was a picture of a woman with a hairstyle from the 1940s standing next to a man wearing an air force uniform. There seemed to be no organization of anything on the desk or any other place in the apartment. Then he spotted what he wanted laying on a blotter in the center of the desk, a worn black wallet. He reached over and flipped it open. Inside he found twenty-seven dollars and a picture of the same woman that was on the wall above the desk. All he wanted was cash so he put the money in his pocket and the wallet back on the desk. Then retreated and silently opened the door of the apartment and checked to see if anyone was in the hallway. When he was sure no one was present he stepped out of the apartment. Checking the other apartments on the floor for an unlocked door was unsuccessful, so he returned to the health center.

When the elevator disgorged the walkers, canes, and scooters back on the third floor after the Mexican fiesta Damien and Millie followed the parade back toward their respective apartments. Reaching for her keys Millie said, "Damien you still owe me $4.95 for the medicine I picked up for you at Walgreens."

"I`ll get it for you right now, so I won`t forget" he replied. Opening his door he went in and came back quickly holding his wallet. "Millie, my money`s gone!" he said showing her the empty wallet.

"Are you sure you had it? You know how forgetful you can be."

"I know it was there because I checked this afternoon to see if I would have lunch money for tomorrow."

"I noticed that your door was unlocked. How many times have I told you about that?" she scolded him.

"I know, I know." an admonished Damien replied. "But somebody stole my money."

The time and the place for Raymond`s meeting with Tom was 9:00 P.M.at the back of the apartment building next to the grotto of the Blessed Virgin. Watching from the back entrance instead of Slick Johnnie`s pink pimpmobile Raymond saw a black Cadillac Escalade pull up and a rear window open. Walking over he saw an oriental looking face looking out and he said, "I'm Raymond. Are you Tom?"

The voice he recognized from the phone call said, "Yes, I`m Tom. Do you have the cash?"

Raymond replied, "I have the money do you have my order?"

"Hand it over first. Then you get your drugs."

Raymond handed Tom what money he had and Tom counted it. "This isn`t nearly enough you weasel! You don`t pay attention. Payment in full or no merchandise." He handed Raymond a piece of paper with a phone number on it and added, "Call that number when you have the cash."

The window rolled up and the black Cadillac drove off.

Raymond stood there in his blue scrubs and combat boots and began to shiver. All the warmth and confidence he felt earlier that day had vanished. What I do now, he thought. Nick the janitor, his best customer will be here soon looking for the heroin for himself and his girlfriend.

Going back into the building he walked up to the third floor, but instead of going to the nursing wing he turned and entered the chapel.

Approaching the life size statue of the Blessed Virgin, he grasped it by the base and slid it sideways on the pedestal revealing the deep depression of an old holy water font. Reaching in he pulled out a grimy plastic bag. Opening the bag he checked to see if all his fentanyl pills from Granny`s drug business were still there. They were and he knew the fentanyl was the strong stuff that could put some people on an eternal trip. He also knew that Nick and his girlfriend were long time heroin users and could handle the new drug. He counted out twenty-eight pills. A one week supply for Nick and his girlfriend. He would have to charge them a lot more now since the cost of doing business had gone up.

CHAPTER

14

The following Monday in the squad room at the Zone One headquarters, Detective Lakeisha Johnson walked over from the copy machine and handed Cash a report on two overdoses in the Holy Angels parking lot from two nights previously. "The guy was a janitor at Holy Angels and the female was his live-in girlfriend. We know it was fentanyl, because they had a baggie with a number of pills in it and the lab confirmed that`s what they were."

LaKeisha stood at his desk and continued, "Let me think. That makes three confirmed cases there and one questionable case with the football player".

"Who was the third case?" Cash asked.

"I got a call from the administrator at Holy Angels that there is a lawsuit filed against them by the mother of one of the ninety-five year old residents in the nursing unit, who died from a fentanyl overdose confirmed by autopsy. She wants me to check out that football player again."

"Why would anyone want to do an autopsy on a ninety-five year old in a nursing home?'

"Her daughter claimed that there were several sudden overnight deaths in the nursing unit over the last couple of months with no plausible cause of death noted."

"I`m free this afternoon," Cash said, "And this could end up as a homicide. Why don`t I come along and see what kind of bag of worms you are opening. Let`s catch some lunch first. Do you have any place you`d like to go?"

"There`s a snitch of mine, who has some info on the on the Korean muscle. He`s supposed to meet me up on Wylie Avenue. I`ll treat you to some real soul food."

Fifteen minutes later, they walked into Big Mama`s Soul Food Emporium. Cash knew he would be the only white face in the crowd and he wondered if his Native American genes would give him any street credibility.

Big Mamma was behind the cash register and when she saw Lakeisha she moved her massive body around the counter and gave Lakeisha a big hug and said, "What brings you up on the hill, Detective?"

"It`s your fantastic food, Big Mama, and I need to teach this paleface how to enjoy soul food." She then introduced Cash.

"Well, Detective Cash you came to the right place. We are gonna fatten you up a bit."

Lakeisha asked for a table up front, so she could watch the door. After they were seated and placed the order, Cash realized that everyone had stopped staring at him. So he felt comfortable enough to ask who was this guy who wanted to talk with her.

"His name is Rudolph, and he`s a former addict, I helped him out one time by talking to the judge about probation rather than jail time. Basically he`s a runner for a local loan shark, so he knows who owes who and how much." About this time, Cash was confronted with a massive amount of food that would have fed his airborne unit in Afghanistan for a month. He and Lakeisha dug in and about half-way through the meal, a tall skinny man in an oversized black hoodie stopped outside the front door. He looked nervously up and down Wylie Avenue and then quickly entered the restaurant. He spotted Lakeisha who motioned him to come to their table.

"Pull up a chair Rudolph so we can talk."

Shifting back and forth on his feet as though he was a little kid who needed to go to the bathroom he pointed at Cash and asked, "Is he o.k.?" Lakeisha nodded. So Rudolph sat down and continued, "The Koreans is squeezing all the dealers. Everybody is cryin` for money. They are really mean guys. They be the ones that gunned down that Northside dealer. That`s all I have for you now."

Lakeisha smiled and said, "Let me know if you hear anything more. " She then palmed a twenty dollar bill and put it under a napkin on the table. It disappeared into Rudolph`s pocket and he disappeared out the front door.

Pushing away from the table, Cash said, "Well that confirms your suspicion of s drug war, LaKeisha. What do we do next?"

"First of all, we go to Holy Angels and find out if there really is a fentanyl problem there."

Having seen Cash push back from the table Big Mama came rushing over and asked, "How about some sweet potato pie?"

Suppressing a belch, Cash put his hands up in surrender and politely declined. Lakeisha also declined and pushing her chair back stood up. Cash did likewise and asked for the check. Big Mama smiled and taking Cash`s hand said, "Paleface, anytime Detective Johnson brings a guest it`s on the house."

Driving back to the Northside LaKeisha asked what he thought of the meal.

"Fantastic!! The breaded fatback with cornmeal bread was the best followed by the Hoppin John as a side dish. All in all at this point, I would prefer to take a nap than go to Holy Angels."

CHAPTER

15

Marilyn Cassidy, the Executive Director, was waiting at the reception desk for the detectives as Phillip Cash and LaKeisha Johnson walked by the concrete angel guards at the front entrance and entered the lobby of Holy Angels. Marilyn was dressed in a similar business suit that LaKeisha had remembered from their last meeting. Extending her hand to LaKeisha she said, "Thanks for coming over on short notice. I really appreciate it."

Taking her hand in a soft manner, she replied, "Not a problem investigation is what we do." She introduced Cash and added "Detective Cash is with the homicide unit and it looks like Holy Angels may have a problem in that area."

"I`m not sure what`s going on. Let`s go to my office and talk. Maybe you can help us get to the bottom of this." She turned and started walking down the hall to the right. Arriving there she opened the door and ushered the two detectives in. As they entered, Jeannie Edwards arose to meet them and she nodded to LaKeisha. Marilyn Cassidy then introduced Detective Cash to Jeannie reiterating that Cash was from the homicide unit.

After they all were seated, LaKeisha began, "From our phone conversation you said one of your residents died suddenly overnight in the nursing unit several weeks ago and the daughter demanded an autopsy. When the report came back that the cause of death was a fentanyl overdose the daughter threatened Holy Angels with a lawsuit."

"That's right Detective, but my first question is the lab report accurate?'

LaKeisha took the initiative. "Our lab guys are really good and they are getting plenty of experience with the current drug problems." She continued "Opioids, both prescription and street drugs are everywhere. We need to know if they are here in your retirement community and how they got here."

Cash entered the conversation with, "You had two overdoses in your parking lot Saturday night. One of the deceased was an employee here. You had and another questionable overdosing with the football player episode. So I agree that as you said, we need to get to the bottom of this." He continued "What is the story about the sudden unexplained deaths in the nursing unit."

At this point Marilyn appeared to be a little flustered and confused, "That's why I asked Mrs. Edwards to come to the meeting. Jeannie would you please tell us what you know."

A consummate professional Jeannie responded, " First, the unexpected sudden deaths. In the last three months we have had four deaths on our unit. The first death was an eighty-six year old male who died from lung cancer. In early October a ninety-five year old female with a long history of heart disease ate lunch, sat back in her bed, and died from a cardiac arrest. She had a DNR form on her chart, so no resuscitation was performed. The other two deaths were unexpected. On October twenty-ninth, an eighty-six year old female died at 12:23

A.M. for no apparent reason. She was a diabetic who had an ulcer on her right ankle and was doing well at bed rest. The fourth death was on November fifteenth, an 84 year old female, who had cataract surgery in her only good eye that day, and was here for an overnight stay. She was found dead on midnight rounds. I have the charts here if you would like to review them." Mrs. Edwards, can make copies for you" Marilyn volunteered. "'Jeannie, tell them about the nursing notes the night of the alleged overdose."

"The night of that incident, the story is that Mrs. Bailey told me was that our night orderly had come into her room and given her a new blood pressure pill that the doctor had called in. She took the pill and felt like she was having an out of body experience and seeing flashing colored lights. The next thing she remembered was seeing her friends standing at the bedside. The thing that concerned me was that there was no doctor`s order on the chart for a new blood pressure medication. I`m sure of that because I`m the only R.N. on duty to take a doctor`s order"

Cash interrupted to ask, "Did you check with the doctor to see if he had called in an order for an additional medicine?"

"Yes, I did and the answer was no".

Cash continued "My understanding is that orderlies cannot give out medications. Is that correct?"

"You are correct."

"Then it looks like we need to talk with that orderly again."

"That`s Raymond Benson, " the Executive Director offered. "He`s not due to report for work until 4 P.M. Would you like his home address?"

"We already have it, but let Mr. Benson know that we will be contacting him again. Are the other residents here today that were present the night of the Narcan incident? We would like to ask them a few more questions."

By this point, Marilyn Cassidy knew that she was way over her head and responded, "I don't know. I just don't know. Let me have the receptionist check and see if the residents are available."

After getting the doctor's name, address, and phone number for the detectives Marilyn checked with the receptionist and told the detectives that Mrs. Estel and Mrs. Bailey were available and on their way down. Mr. Skrcyzinski was not in his room. Marilyn offered her office for the questioning and poured the two detectives some coffee. At this point Jeannie Edwards said that if there were no more questions for her that she would be leaving. Both detectives thanked her for the information she had provided. LaKeisha handed her a business card and asked her to call if she thought of anything more that might be helpful. When Mrs. Estel and Mrs. Bailey arrived, the Executive Director escorted them in and then she conducted the introductions and excused herself. As she was leaving she said, "Detectives, Holy Angels desperately needs your help."

The questioning of Millie Estel and Rita Bailey did not uncover any new information. However both ladies agreed, Damien Skrcyzinski was only defending Millie in the Narcan episode and he never would try to hurt anyone intentionally.

CHAPTER

16

After Cash and Lakeisha left Holy Angels, they called Raymond with the phone number Marilyn Cassidy had given them. He answered with his usual, "Yeah." When he heard that they wanted to talk to him again. He said he didn`t have time to talk and hung up.

The thought of talking to the police a second time confused and unnerved Raymond and he decided that he needed a plan. The cops are suspicious about the fentanyl he thought but they will never find it. Maybe he would have to move on to some warm place, but he needed to get even with that big SOB first. To clear his mind, he went to the refrigerator and took out the last can of Iron City Beer. Opening it he flopped back on the couch. After 20 minutes of racking his brain and nothing of substance was forthcoming, so he decided to prime the pump with some meth. Reaching under the seat cushion of the couch, he pulled out a baggie and popped one of his dwindling supply of pills into his mouth and swallowed it with more beer.

Getting up he put on his warm socks, combat boots, quilted jacket and Elmer Fudd hat and set out for Taco Bell. The cold air and meth sharpened his mind by the time he got there. Eating inside at one of the tables he hatched what he thought was a brilliant plan to deflect any suspicions the cops had about him and also how to get even with the big football player.

About ten that evening, the desk sergeant at Zone One head-quarters got an anonymous phone call that the cops should check the football player's room at Holy Angels for fentanyl. Texting this to LaKeisha`s cell phone, she immediately picked up and reading the message she contacted Cash. "With the episode of suspected fentanyl overdose and a proven death at Holy Angels we have probable cause to get a search warrant," she told him.

"You pick out the judge and I`ll take the paperwork over first thing in the morning and get it to him in his chamber before court begins."

"You got it, Cash." she answered "Let me know when you have the warrant ready and we`ll both go to Holy Angels."

December fourth at seven-forty A.M., Cash, LaKeisha, and two uniformed officers arrived at Damien`s apartment. Knocking on the door Cash announced their arrival. Damien responded with, "Come on in it`s unlocked."

Opening the door cautiously they saw Damien sitting on a couch watching television. Stepping into the apartment Cash crossed the room and presented the warrant. The others came in behind him.

Damien saw the uniformed officers and stood up. Holding the warrant in his right hand he asked, "I don`t understand what this is all about?"

Cash said, "Please sit back down, Mr. Skrcyzinski. The warrant is permission for us to search your apartment."

"What are you looking for?"

"We`ll let you know when we find it."

Within a matter of two minutes, LaKeisha was holding up a baggie she had found in a desk drawer. Inside the baggie were some light brown pills. Showing it to Damien she asked "What`s this?"

Looking at the bag in her hand he said, "I don`t know. It`s not mine."

"Well how did it get there if it`s not yours?"

"I don`t know."

After another 15 minutes of searching the apartment nothing else of interest was found.

"We need you to come down to the station and answer some more questions" Cash advised him.

"Okay, but do I have time to go to the skilled nursing unit to help with breakfast. Some of the older people have trouble feeding themselves and I help with the trays."

"I`m sure that the older folks will get something to eat without your help. As of right now, you are officially under arrest for possession of illegal drugs. Let`s go."

After hand cuffing Damien one of the uniformed officers put Damien`s overcoat over his shoulders and the procession marched out past the concrete guardian angels and headed for the Zone One station house.

CHAPTER
17

The breakfast clatter was winding down in the skilled nursing care unit at Holy Angels Retirement Community, as Millie Estel collected the trays from the patients rooms. As a volunteer in the nursing care unit, this had been her morning ritual that had been going on for more than three years since she had moved into apartment 371 at Holy Angels.

Millie is an eighty- six year old widow and mother of four grown children. She had been the bread winner in the family and she had to work full time to support and educate her brood. She had also been active in church activities and was the neighborhood air raid warden during World War II. Now that she is in a retirement community, she dedicated her time to helping the "old folks."

Now that her chores were finished, she left the nursing care unit and headed for her special place of serenity, a small chapel on the same floor as the nursing unit. She sat down on one of the benches and she was at peace with herself and the world. The soft pastel blue walls and the sun shining through a stained-glass window made this an ideal place for quiet meditation. After a few moments, Millie got up and as she left the chapel she stopped to admire the simplicity of the this special place. Then it was off to meet Rita and Damien her best friends for breakfast. She took the elevator to the first floor rather than the steps, as part of her condescendence to her 86 years on this planet. As the elevator opened, she walked down the long hall to the brightly lit cafeteria. The dinner menu had already been posted and as advertised today was an ethnic day that featured Italian cuisine. Italian wedding soup, two different pasta dishes and spumoni for dessert were promised and would be well received by the residents. Millie spotted Rita who was already there at their usual table. Valerie and Warren were also seated at the same table. Millie went over to the service bar and filled her bowl with cream of wheat and added a few cranberries. She found an empty chair at the table and joined the group. "How are all the movers and shakers this lovely morning?" she asked. Warren said, "Fair to middling," Rita agreed with that assessment and Valerie nodded her approval. "Has anyone seen Damien this morning? He never misses helping at breakfast in the nursing unit." Warren opined Damien liked to stay up late some nights to watch the old gangster movies in black and white on Turner Classic Movies. "Maybe he just overslept," Valerie offered.

Just then Millie's cell phone beeped and she excused herself to pick up the call. "What!! Where is he? I can`t believe this. I`ll be there as soon as I can."

"Millie, what was that all about?" asked Rita.

"Damien is in the city jail and he won`t talk to anyone there. The detective I talked to says Damien is in big trouble and refuses to get a lawyer until he talks to me".

Pushing his chair back Warren said" I'll get my car and drive you. The jail is on Brighton Road just off North Avenue."

"I'm going too" said Rita.

Valerie chimed in, "We'll all go. If Damien is in trouble, he needs all the help he can get. Wait for me I have to get my walker."

After loading the walker into the trunk, the four octogenarians all piled into a faded silver blue 2006 Lincoln town car which had two missing hub caps and set off for the trip down North Avenue toward Zone One headquarters and the city jail.

Zone One headquarters and the city jail were situated in a drab concrete building on Brighton Avenue. At one time the façade was a bright gray color but the many years of the smog before pollution control had turned it to this grimy gray foreboding monstrosity.

Warren pulled into a handicapped parking space in the front row of the parking lot. He pulled the blue plastic handicapped sticker out of the glove compartment and hung it on the rearview mirror. Millie and her gang exited the town car and entered the building. She approached the desk manned by Sargent O'Connor and she announced that they were there to help Damien. After a few questions the Sargent asked them to be seated and made a brief phone call.

The intercom in the squad room barked out, "Hey Cash, it looks like you have the entire old folks home waiting for you out here in the lobby." Detective Phillip Cash put on his jacket and tightened his tie and went down to the front desk. After Introducing himself to the group a five-minute discussion convinced him that Millie would be the one he wanted to interview and after that she would be the only one allowed to talk to Damien.

Cash led the group to a waiting area where a bail bonds man was explaining to a distraught woman about how much it will cost to bond her husband out of jail. The detective made sure the other octogenarians would be comfortable, and had Millie follow him to an interview room as drab as the exterior of the building. Detective Cash offered

Millie a seat and he took a place behind a small desk, "Mrs. Estel, please tell me what you know about Mr. Skrcyzinski."

"Please Detective Cash just call me Millie and before we go any further, can you tell me why is Damien in jail?"

"As you surely know there have been several unusual deaths at the Holy Angels Home, and Mr. Skrcyzinski is a person of interest and we have evidence that makes a strong case that he may be involved."

"Are you saying that Damien could be responsible for those deaths?"

"No. We are just gathering more information at this point. So please tell me what you can about Mr. Skrcyzinski and his background."

"Well, I knew him when he was an altar boy at St. Mary`s Church here on the Northside. I was a lector at that time and he was just a nice young boy. I know he was a big football star in high school and college. You know he , played for the Steelers. When he moved into Holy Angels Retirement Community about a year and a half ago, he recognized me immediately and we resumed our friendship. His apartment is two doors from mine, and I see him in the nursing care unit at Holy Angels every morning. He helps with breakfast for the old folks. He is a very nice and gentle man and very big. What else would you like to know?"

"Why will he only talk to you and not a lawyer?"

"Well, he tends to get confused at times and has trouble with his memory. We have a lot of activities at Holy Angels and he gets times and dates mixed up, so I help him with things like that. In addition, as I said, he volunteers with me every morning in the care unit with me and then we have breakfast together".

"Millie, he is six feet seven inches and weighs about two hundred and eighty pounds and has a history of violent outbursts doesn`t that concern you?"

"Well, I`m four feet. ten inches and weigh eighty-eight pounds and no, it doesn`t worry me at all. He would never hurt anyone. He is my friend."

"Has he ever talked to you about his past?"

"Yes, at times, he has. When he was in grade school he suffered a serious emotional upset. This was during World War II and his father was a tail gunner in a B-17 bomber. His plane went down on a bombing mission and crashed into the Black Sea. There were no survivors. Damien was devastated. He idolized his father and has pictures of him and his father`s plane hanging in his room. Since he was an only child his father had told Damien to take care of his mother, while he was gone. Damien was only in the second grade at the time, but took this responsibility seriously.

Of course, his mother Mary was also devastated. So now she was a single parent she needed to work and raise her son. She sacrificed and tried to be both a mother and father to him. In high school, he was a football star and had multiple scholarship offers.

At this point, he told his mother that as the man of the family he was going to get a job loading beer trucks at the local beer distributor, and she could retire. Well of course his mother would have none of that and insisted he attend college. Is that enough background for you, Detective?"

"That certainly helps. What about anything in later life? Did he ever talk about that?"

"He was married at one time and he and his wife had a lovely young daughter. Unfortunately, they both were killed in a tragic automobile accident. He never discussed any of the details of the accident with me . As I mentioned earlier, his memory does have lapses. He was proud when he signed a contract with the Steelers. He was able to move his mother to a small home of her own in Dormont."

"What about his present activities? He told me that he was a heavy drinker."

"I don't t know that is the correct term? He ran into a former Steeler a while back, who helped Damien to come to Holy Angels Retirement Community. This former team mate got him started in Alcoholics Anonymous. I make sure he attends his meetings regularly. I don't think he has had a drink since he came to our community. We have a lot of things to do Holy Angels. He likes to play bingo on Thursdays, he volunteers in the health center for breakfast, and he also pushes wheel chairs around when there are special events. He talks to the older men about football. That's about all I can tell you. Can I talk with Damien now?"

"You said he has not had an alcoholic drink for some time. Mr. Skrcyzinski says that he spends most of his afternoons in a Northside saloon. How do your account for that?"

"I've lived all my life in the same neighborhood before moving to Holy Angels and I know just about everybody on the Northside. Fred is the bartender at the Shamrock Café, and I went down there and told Fred that Damien was in Alcoholics anonymous and to serve him only Doctor Pepper. I think Fred will do it. Fred is a little afraid of me, because Fred's mother and I were classmates in grade school."

"Thank you, Millie, your information will be helpful for our investigation."

Getting up from his chair Detective Cash said, "We can go and have you talk with Mr. Skrcyzinski right now, but please tell him to get a lawyer because he really needs one. May I get you a Coke or something to drink?"

"'A cup of coffee would be fine. No cream or sugar."

When Millie, Rita, and Valerie arrived at the ballroom for Sally`s 1:30 P.M. low impact exercise class that afternoon, they were greeted with a barrage of questions. "What were the police doing on the third floor this morning?" Jennifer Appelt blurted out. Before either of the three women could respond, several more questions were asked from the group of residents crowding around the sign in book. "Let me sign in first and then we can talk," Rita said. Before Rita could finish writing her name in the signup book, another question was asked by one of the growing crowd who wanted to know if it was true that a SWAT team was on the third floor hallway. Another resident volunteered she had heard from one of the ladies in housekeeping there was a drug dealer in the building, and the police were chasing him down the second floor stairway but he got away.

Fortunately for the three women being questioned, Sally, the wellness director, called the class to order and the small crowd dispersed taking their seats. "Let`s start our warmup with some stretching of our shoulders and neck," Sally began. Thirty minutes later when the class was ended, the group of residents trapped Millie, Rita, and Valerie in the ballroom in order to get the latest information, so that they could spread the news of the day. Acting as spokesperson Millie began by saying, "Yes, the police had been on the third floor, and yes, Damien had gone with them to the police station to answer some questions." She added, "No, she had not heard about any SWAT team in the building."

"Well, what about the drug dealer running down back steps? The cleaning lady was sure she had heard that it had happened."

"I don`t have any knowledge of that happening. That`s all I know. "Millie replied.

"What about you Valerie? Do you know anything more about the situation?" one of the more aggressive questioners asked.

"What would I know," Valerie replied. "I only live here."

With that Millie essentially ended the news conference and taking Valerie by the hand and motioning to Rita they three women walked out of the ballroom. The aggressive questioner rushed past them so she could get to the arts and crafts room first, where she could tell her friends about the police running the halls of Holy Angels with their guns drawn.

The other members of the small crowd did likewise scurrying off to different locations to spread their new found scoop to the other residents of Holy Angels Retirement Community.

CHAPTER

18

The next morning sitting at the head of the usual table Millie announced to Damien`s Dwarfs (the name they had been given by some of the residents of Holy Angels), Damien was assigned a public defender and he had been charged with possession of illegal drugs. Because they could only hold him for 24 hours on that charge he would be released that morning. She added, "However, he is a person of interest in the fentanyl overdose case."

Warren a retired heavy equipment operator and widower said, "That sounds like a manslaughter or a murder charge to me."

Rita putting down her coffee pointed out, "From what Millie said he saved my life."

Valerie, an ex-nun, who saved her sanity by leaving the Benedictine order after 18 years of dealing with the chaos of forty or more fourth or fifth graders in one classroom, added, "Damien is a good person and would never be involved in anything like that."

Warren countered with, "Are we really sure of that? He broke that guy`s ribs and was known as a very violent person on the football field."

Valerie looked at Warren and said, "Oh, Warren you sit in your apartment and watch too many reruns of CSI."

"At least I`m not a Pollyanna, spending all my time in the grotto praying." He replied.

Millie stood up and said in an authoritative manner "Dwarfs, Damien needs us and the first order of business is to get him out of jail."

Warren said, "I`ll get the car."

Valerie got her walker and the four octogenarians went out and piled into the faded blue town car with the two missing hubcaps and headed for the station house.

Arriving there once again, Warren pulled into the parking lot and eased into a handicapped spot. He attached the blue plastic handicapped sign on his rearview mirror and they all got out and entered the station.

Millie approached the desk Sergeant and told him that they were there to take Mr. Skrcyzinski home.

The Sergeant made a brief phone call and said, "His paperwork is about done and his lawyer is still with him. If you go down the hall on your left to the next counter, they will take care of things."

Thanking the sergeant the troop proceeded down the hallway where they saw Damien standing facing the counter. Next to him was a young woman wearing a dark business suit, who appeared to be about fifteen years old.

Rita called out, "There`s Damien."

Hearing this Damien turned their way and a big smile appeared on his face and he announced to the young woman, "The Dwarfs are here."

Bending down, Damien gently hugged the ladies and shook Warren's hand. Turning to the young woman he said, "This is my lawyer Eileen. She just got me out of jail."

The young woman smiled and said, "I'm Eileen Dugan from the public defender's office. You must be his friends from Holy Angels. Which one of you is Millie?"

Stepping forward Millie extended her hand and said, "That's me, Ms. Dugan."

Taking Millie's hand Eileen Dugan said, "We have all the paperwork here and I'm starting a file on Mr. Skrcyzinski. He said that you would probably want to do the same, so I had them make copies for you."

"That's very nice of you, but I don't think it will be a very thick file since Damien doesn't use or sell drugs."

"I don't think it's that simple." Eileen Dugan replied. "He still is a person of interest in the fentanyl deaths at Holy Angels. I have a friend at the prosecuting attorney's office and she told me that the case was presented to them and they declined to issue an indictment. They wanted more than the circumstantial evidence they already have."

"What kind of evidence would they want?" Millie asked.

"Something that would be definite proof. Like someone seeing him enter the patient's room just before she died, or his fingerprints in the room."

"Well, that won't happen," Millie stated very firmly "Because Damien didn't do it."

Handing Millie the copies of the paperwork Eileen said, "I hope you're right. Here's my card if you need to contact me."

Turning to Damien his attorney added, "I'll be in touch regarding court dates." Putting the files in her briefcase she turned and walked away.

———————————————

Lieutenant Sam Kalina's Office Zone 1 Police Headquarters - Dec. 6th

At seven-forty -five that morning, Detectives Cash and Johnson were summoned to Lieutenant Sam Kalina's office. A twenty-two year veteran of the force, Kalina was a no nonsense guy, who was respected by the rank and file of his department. At five feet eight inches and one hundred and seventy five pounds, he had a military style brush haircut, he still could take down a perp, and have him cuffed in record time. Befitting his demeanor he got right to the point.

"Cash and Johnson, her honor, the Mayor, called this morning because a reporter from the Pittsburgh Press called her and wanted the mayor's office to comment on the possibility of a drug war and the fentanyl epidemic we have in our lovely city. What do we have for her Honor?"

Cash was not in a good mood this morning because his son's principal had sent a note home that he and Laura needed to come to the principal's office and discuss Brian's behavior in class. Without thinking Cash said, "Tell her Honor to have some more fundraisers with some rich donors and let us do our jobs."

Kalina obviously irritated responded, "Come on, Cash! None of your sarcastic shit! There was another gangland hit late yesterday afternoon in the Hill District and a three year old boy was hit in the leg with a stray bullet. The Mayor has a major wedgie up her ass over this and she wants answers."

LaKeisha Johnson jumped in before Cash could answer, "The hit was on my snitch Rudolph. Apparently someone thought he talked too much."

"I hadn`t heard that. I was off the radar last night with family issues," Cash responded. "Here`s what homicide has, Sam. A suspect with some strong circumstantial evidence, but the prosecutor`s office wants to wait for more evidence. We are working on that now."

"What do you have Johnson?" Kalina asked.

She looked at Cash briefly then back to Kalina, "I talked to the detective from Zone 3 and the hit on Wylie avenue sounds like it was the same guys that took out Slick Johnny. Forensics have some shell casings and will compare them to the ones they found on the North Side. As for a drug war, we`re pretty sure that the Korean mafia, the Khangpae, from New York City is muscling in here. They rule by violence. If the casings match, we may need to mobilize a SWAT team to go after them."

"What about the kid that got shot?" Kalina asked.

She responded, "He went to surgery last night and should do well."

"O.K. you guys. I`ll deal with the Mayor but keep me up to date. You go out and do your thing."

PART TWO

CHAPTER
19

All the "old folks" had been fed and Millie and Damien were stacking the empty meal trays on the service cart in the hallway of the skilled nursing facility. "As soon as we`re finished here, we will have our strategy meeting with the rest of the Dwarfs. I`ll see you there." Millie confided in Damien.

After they left the nursing unit, Millie stopped in the chapel to calm herself down In the serenity of this quiet place and to review in her mind the plan to catch a serial killer. She knew that it would be putting her own life at risk, but the police said they needed more evidence. She had seen this work one time on television on a detective show and she realized that this was real life and not television. All of the Dwarfs would have to perform without error or she could die. Millie got up and left the serenity of the chapel and walked to the elevator at the end of the hallway. She entered the elevator and a note on the wall that announced that tonight`s dinner theme would be a southwestern barbecue. Upon entering the dining area she got her cream of wheat and black coffee at the breakfast counter and joined the Dwarfs at their usual table. Millie sat down and called the meeting to order.

"Valerie and Rita, you start surveillance about 7:00 P.M. in Valerie's room. Remember lights out. Report to me when Raymond leaves the building. Damien and Warren, you are back up on the third floor hallway. Watch through the window and If I don't call you within two minutes of Raymond leaving my room come running with the Narcan. I had to bring Mrs. Edwards in on our plan. She is supplying the Narcan and will make up a fake chart on me and put it in the chart rack. I will be in room 365. Remember to keep your cell phones on. I don't want to make an emergency call and hear your voice telling me to leave a message."

Later that Friday morning in the nursing unit, Jeannie Edwards came in early to have a special meeting with Millie. Millie said to Jeannie, "I know you are taking a big risk with your job here Jeannie, but I think we may just get the evidence to prove Damien is innocent and find the real killer."

"What do you want for an admitting diagnosis Millie? "

"How about congestive heart failure?"

"That will work fine. Why don't you get your nightgown and a robe. I'll put an oxygen tank in the room to make it look good and then we will get you 'admitted'."

About 9:00 P.M. that evening Millie got the call, "It's Rita. Raymond just left the building. Just a second, a big black car just pulled into the employees lot." Turning to her co-surveillance partner Rita continued. "What are they doing Valerie? I can't see clearly because of my cataracts."

Turning her attention back to the phone, she told Millie, "Valerie says that Raymond got a bag of something from someone in the car and just went to the grotto. Now he is heading back to the building and the car just left."

"Good work, girls" Millie said and hung up.

As per routine, Jeannie Edwards left the nursing unit at 9:00 to make her rounds in the memory care wing.

At 9:35, Raymond entered room 365 with a small paper cup. Going over to Millie's bedside he said, "Your doctor just called in an order for another heart pill" and handed her the cup with a pill in it.

Millie questioned him, "That`s unusual. Are you sure about it?"

"Listen, lady" he said, "Your doctor wants you to have it tonight and I`m going to make sure you take it."

Millie removed the pill from the cup and pointed to a glass of water sitting on a table at the foot of the bed asked Raymond to hand it to her. As he turned to get the water, Millie adroitly palmed the new "heart pill" and substituted a baby aspirin that she had in her left hand. Making it obvious that she had a pill in her hand she put the baby aspirin in her mouth. She then took the glass from Raymond and swallowed the baby aspirin.

Putting the glass down she said, "Thank you, Raymond."

His response was, "I hope you sleep well tonight."

After Raymond had left she pulled her cell phone from under the covers and called Warren. "Phase 1 of our plan worked perfectly. Let the others know they can stand down. After Raymond goes off duty, I will disappear for a day or two".

Zone 1 Police Headquarters – December 7, 2018, 8:05A.M.

The intercom crackled in the squad room, "Cash, the old folks home is here again and they say they need to talk to you."

When Cash arrived down at the front desk, Millie triumphantly handed him a zip-lock bag with a glass tumbler inside and a baggie with a single light brown pill in it. She said, "Detective Cash you wanted more evidence. Here it is."

Being more than a little confused he said to her, "Let`s go to a room where we can talk." As he started to walk toward an empty interrogation room the whole entourage follows. "No! No! No! Only Millie." The chastised members of the group watched as Cash and Millie entered an interview room and he closed the door.

After Millie`s ten minute explanation of their plan Cash skeptically said, "You are telling me that five people in the home all of whom are in their eighties and nineties have decided some guy they don`t like is a serial killer and he tried to kill you last night and you want me to arrest him."

"First of all, Detective Cash, it is not The Home. It is Holy Angels Retirement Community. All we want you to do is run the fingerprints on the national data base and also determine if that pill is fentanyl. We don`t think Raymond Benson is really Raymond Benson, and Warren says this is how they catch a lot of criminals on television."

Cash slumped back in his chair and looked up at the ceiling said, "O.K. I`ll do it, but don`t expect miracles."

Millie smiled and said, "While you check the evidence, we can pray to the Blessed Virgin for a miracle if you need any help."

Suppressing a smile Cash got up and led Millie back to the waiting group.

When they were all back in the car everyone began to talk at once. After Millie answered all of their questions one by one. Warren asked "Now, you said that you needed to disappear at your sister`s for a few days, I can drive you there right now if you give me her address."

CHAPTER

20

December 12, 2018

Phil and Laura Cash were finished with dinner and sat in the living room of their one-hundred- year old two-story red brick home in the Fineview area of Pittsburgh. Fineview was obviously named for the fine view of the panorama of the city. From the picture window in the living room, the view encompassed the lower Northside, then across the busy Allegheny River to a bustling downtown. The vista extended southward across the Monongahela River to Mount Washington. Turning to the west you could see the confluence of the Allegheny and Monongahela Rivers to form the mighty Ohio River. Indeed it was a fine view

They sipped the last of their coffees and reviewed the day. Robin, their ten year old daughter had triumphantly shown them her artwork depicting the Pilgrims and native Americans enjoying the first Thanksgiving. She prominently placed the Native Americans in her drawing and had told the teacher that she and her father were part Native American.

Brian the six year old was doing fine academically, but still was a disruptive presence in the classroom and school yard. How to deal with this was the current discussion. Just then the phone rang and Phil went to the kitchen and picked up the call. It was Henry Kim, their neighbor from across the street, "Phil, I hate to bother you at home but my family needs your advice and help. Do you have a few minutes to talk?"

"Sure, Henry, what can I help you with?"

"I`d rather not talk about it on the phone. Can I come over to your place and talk?"

"Absolutely! We`ve just finished eating. Come on over."

A few minutes later Henry and Phil sat at in the living room, while Laura was cleaning up in the kitchen. She stuck her head into the room and greeted Henry and asked if he would like a cup of coffee. He declined and she retreated back to the kitchen.

"So what`s the problem?" Phil asked.

"There is a serious threat to the safety of my parents and by extension to me and my wife and children."

Phil took a sip of his now cold coffee and sat back and indicated to Henry to continue.

"As you know, my parents have a small restaurant downtown on Sixth Avenue. Last evening about nine o`clock as they were cleaning up and preparing to close for the night, a young Korean woman came running in and asked them to hide her. She was hysterical, but the story she gave was almost unbelievable." Henry sat back and took a deep breath.

"Go on," Phil prodded.

"She claimed that she had been kidnapped in the small village of Bupyung in South Korea and smuggled into the U.S. and forced into prostitution by Korean criminals." Henry paused here to organize his thoughts and continued. "She was brought into downtown Pittsburgh to a cheap hotel and a Korean thug arranged for her to meet a John in the lobby. The John came and had obviously been drinking. The thug turned her over to that man, who pushed her down a hallway and into a room. The first thing the guy did was to go into the bathroom. She bolted from the room and ran out the back door of the hotel. She ran frantically, but had no idea where she was. Somehow she ended up on Sixth Avenue and ran past my parent`s restaurant. She saw the menu in the window written in English and Korean. My mother had just put a small nativity scene in the front window of the restaurant that morning, so the young woman knew that they were Christians and would help her. My father was setting the tables for the next day, and the woman ran to him and literally collapsed in his arms. My mother heard the commotion and came out of the kitchen to investigate. They managed to have the woman sit on a chair and tried to get an explanation, but all the woman would say was that evil men had kidnapped her and made her do bad things. My mother took her back into the kitchen and tried to calm her down with a cup of tea. My Dad went out to lock the front door just as three burly Koreans pushed their way in. Dad told them that the restaurant was closed for the night. They pushed him aside and asked if a young girl had come in. He said that no one had been by and the last diners had left forty-five minutes earlier." Henry took a deep breath at this point and said, "I think I need that coffee now."

Phil got up and went into the kitchen and returned with the coffee.

After taking a sip Henry sat back and said, "Thanks for the coffee and thanks for listening to my story."

Phil sat down "Please continue."

"Well, the thugs didn`t believe him and they came in and began to search the place. After they finished in the main dining room, if you remember, there is a small upstairs private dining room. They went up there cursing and not being too careful with any of the furnishings. Next, they came down and burst into the kitchen. My mother was doing some dishes and they confronted her. She must be a great actress because she didn`t appear nervous at all and would talk to them only in Korean. They trashed most of the kitchen but could find no trace of the girl. They finally stood my parents up against the kitchen wall and warned them if they found out that they were lying their restaurant would be burned down. Then, they walked out cursing and turning over tables on their way."

"Where was the girl?" Phil asked.

"My mother heard them come in and hid the girl in a storage cabinet under a sink."

"So is she is still in the restaurant?"

"No." he paused then added "She`s across the street in my basement with my parents. Phil, we need your help."

Detective Phillip Cash sat back took another sip of his cold coffee and realized that he was now wearing two hats. One was that of a neighbor and friend. The other was that of a policeman sworn to uphold the law.

Pushing back from the table he said, "Let me check with Laura and make sure the kids are getting ready for bed. Then, I`d like to go over and talk to your parents and this girl." Going into the den he saw that Brian had already put on his pajamas and Laura was checking Robin`s science homework with her. Laura looked up and asked what the problem was. Cash said, "I`m going over to Henry`s for a while we can talk later."

A few minutes later Phil and Henry walked down the steps to Henry`s finished basement. There was a large couch, several easy chairs, and a large screen television set. A door was open to a small guest bedroom. Sitting on the couch were Henry`s parents and Henry`s wife, Hilda. In one of the easy chairs was a small Korean girl in high heels, a short yellow low-cut dress, and too much makeup. Phil guessed her to be about nineteen years old. Immediately, Henry`s parents stood up and bowed. But the Korean girl remained seated looking at the floor. Hilda, Henry`s wife, also got up and greeted Phil.

Phil walked over and shaking the father`s hand he turned to the mother and in broken Korean said, "*An nyeong ha se yo*."

She relied in perfect English, "Thanks for coming to help us." Turning to the girl, she helped her stand and told Phil, "This is Soon Ling Oh." The girl partially bowed and Phil nodded back. Then Henry pulled up two chairs for Phil and himself and they all sat down.

The girl spoke in halting English and a forty-five minute discussion followed about her ordeal, as she traveled from Bup Yung South Korea and how she arrived at the Kim`s Garden of the Morning Calm Korean Restaurant in Pittsburgh, Pennsylvania. She broke down sobbing several times telling how she and two other girls had been abused and mistreated by their captors.

Later that evening, when Phil crossed the street to his home he found Laura up waiting for him in the den. Phil recounted to her the amazing story, he had just heard over in his neighbor`s basement. Laura somewhat astounded asked him, "What do the Kim`s want you to do?"

"They don`t know what they want me to do, and frankly at this point, I`m not sure what I want to do."

CHAPTER
21

Very early the next morning Phil Cash, Henry Kim`s father, and Soon Ling Oh, got into Cash`s two thousand sixteen Chevy Malibu and started down the hill from Fineview heading on an exploratory expedition. They crossed the Sixth Street bridge went crosstown to the Liberty Bridge and into the Liberty Tubes that went under Mount Washington. Exiting the tunnel they turned left onto route fifty one south. What Cash was trying to reproduce was the route the thugs had taken when they drove Soon Ling to the downtown hotel.

During the discussion the prior evening in Henry Kim`s basement, Soon Ling had told the group that she and two other South Korean Girls were being held prisoners in a two-story house overlooking a river. She did not know the name of the river or the town where they were being held captive. However she did say that there was a large abandoned building and next to it was a large rusty structure that resembled a giant beer barrel. Further along during the previous night's meeting, she described her trip into downtown Pittsburgh. Three of the thugs had taken her in a large black vehicle to the hotel. At first they just drove along the river and then took a road that came to a tunnel where they made a right turn. It was a long brightly lit tunnel that opened to a bridge where they crossed the river and were in a big city.

Reversing this story Cash thought the place where the girls were being held was on the south side of the Monongahela River, somewhere along the western Pennsylvania Rust Belt. It was a long shot but he had to start somewhere. The abandoned building she described sounded like an abandoned steel mill with a huge Bessemer converter next to it.

Driving south they exited route fifty-one and merged onto Pennsylvania route eight-thirty-nine that ran along parallel to the Monongahela River. The sun had come out and the river flatlands on either side blended into wooded hillsides with the stark out lines of bare winter branches at the crest of the hills. The small towns they drove through showed the economic blight that had occurred with the demise of the steel mills after World War II; boarded up stores stood next to pawn shops and saloons.

Nothing seemed remotely familiar to Soon Ling, and Cash was beginning to think how futile this expedition was. He thought we have the chance of a snowball in hell and it might take some kind of miracle to find the other girls. They drove through the town of Monongahela and on to Donora twenty-four miles south east of Pittsburgh. Donora was the town that in 1948 experienced the worst smog disaster in our nation`s history. With a population of fourteen thousand, twenty people died from the thermal inversion that also caused a wall of smog that produced over six thousand cases of respiratory problems. Another fifty people died of respiratory diseases in the following months. The main employers in the area at that time were the American Steel and Wire Plant, as well as U.S. Steel`s Donora Zinc Works.

As they came over a rise in the terrain Cash mused that the only other thing that Donora was famous for was that it was the birthplace of Stan Musial the Saint Louis Cardinals hall of fame slugger. Looking toward the river he saw the remnants of the once bustling industrial areas.

Soon Ling suddenly grabbed the now dozing Mr. Kim and began chattering excitedly in Korean to him. Cash slowed down and asked what she was saying. Mr. Kim replied, "She says that`s it. It`s what she could see from the second story of the house where they are being held." About fifty yards ahead Cash pulled the Malibu into the parking lot of a twenty-four hour laundromat and parked facing the abandoned factory with a Bessemer converter next to it. Cash just sat there and marveled that indeed the converter did look somewhat like a giant rusty beer barrel. The converter stood almost four stories high and dwarfed an abandoned stake truck parked in the empty lot next to it. Cash did not know much about the steel making process but he did remember that the Bessemer process was the method used for the mass production of steel from molten pig iron.

Tears began to run down Soon Ling`s cheeks and she began to shake. Mr. Kim put his arm around her shoulder and in a soft voice began to comfort her in their native language.

"Ask her if she`s sure that this is what she could see from the house."

After conversing for a brief time with her Mr. Kim said, "Yes she`s sure because of the giant beer barrel. She also said that the house where she was held must be higher up on one of these hills. "Cash backed the car up and pulled out of the parking lot onto the road and drove to the first intersection and turned up the hill away from the river. After several blocks he turned left on to a side street that had old pickup trucks in the driveways and car ports. He stopped by an empty lot where they could again view the factory. Soon Ling agreed that this was about the correct distance from the beer barrel, but they should go further on the side street to get a better alignment with what she remembered. Cash proceeded slowly ahead and the houses became fewer and fewer. Soon Ling did not recognize anything familiar on this street. Cash stopped and asked her if there was anything else she remembered seeing.

After some brief thought she said that there was a house with green shingles on the roof. The house was on a street down the hill from where she was kept captive. Cash got out of the car and looking up and down the hillside he looked for green shingles. Because all the trees were bare this time of year it aided his search. Looking further up the hill side he spotted green shingles and on the street one block higher was a two story red brick house.

Getting back in the car he made a U-turn and headed back to the main road and turned up the hill arriving at the street with the two story house. He advised Soon Ling to get down and away from the window and then he turned onto the street and drove by at a normal residential speed. Sitting in the driveway and appearing out of place in this neighborhood was a two thousand eighteen black Cadillac Escalade with tinted windows. Cash continued to the next intersection and turned down the hill. Then he turned onto the street with the house that had the green shingles. He had Soon Ling sit up and told her to get a good look at the two story house as he drove by on the street below it. Soon Ling excitedly confirmed that she was certain that this was the house where she had been held hostage with the other two girls. She recognized the house because of the scalloped blue curtains in the second floor windows.

Satisfied with this, Cash did not want to elicit any suspicion with a relatively new car patrolling the neighborhood so he turned down the hill and headed back to the Northside. On the way back, he mused that maybe miracles still could happen.

CHAPTER
22

After dropping off the elder Mr. Kim and Soon Ling Oh at Henry Kim`s house, Cash headed for Zone One headquarters. He called Detective LaKeisha Johnson on her cell phone and when she answered He told her, "We need to meet somewhere that we can talk privately."

"Sounds serious."

"It is and I will explain it when I see you. How about the Burger King on the corner in about ten minutes?"

"You got it."

Cash disconnected. LaKeisha was his closest friend in the department and a good listener.

She arrived first and had a table in the back with two cups of coffee waiting. Cash went back and pulled out a chair. He thanked her for coming and sat down.

"This doesn`t sound like your six year old son misbehaving at school. What`s going on?" she asked.

Adding a little cream to his coffee, he began to stir it and looking directly into her eyes began, "I`ve stumbled into an international human trafficking cartel that may involve the Korean Mafia that you think is muscling into the narcotics trade here in town."

LaKeisha looking directly back at him said, "We could have talked about this in the squad room. Why the secrecy?"

"Because I`m way out of my Jurisdiction and I`m way in over my head." Cash continued starting with Henry Kim`s basement meeting and then relating the story of Soon Ling Oh. He told her about how she was at a singles bar in Incheon with some of her friends and met three clean cut young Korean men. As the night went on they moved to a house party and it sounds, like Rohypnol, commonly referred to as a roofie, the date rape drug, was involved. The drug can last up to eight hours and nothing can be remembered while under the influence. The next thing she remembered was that she and two other girls were on a ship out to sea. Cash stopped and took a sip of his coffee. LaKeisha sat in silence and indicated with her hand for him to continue.

"The crew of the ship were all Koreans and they treated the girls with deference. They fed them and let them out on deck, but otherwise had no contact with them. After several days at sea, they docked at a small port. The girls had no idea where they were. Once they were on shore they were met by the same young men that were in the singles bar in Incheon. They were roughly pushed into the back of a delivery van and driven inland to a small airfield where they boarded a two engine plane with their captors. By this time, they had recognized some signs in Spanish and guessed they were in Mexico or South America." Cash paused at this point and took a deep breath.

"After a short flight, they landed in a desolate field where a large van was waiting. Once they got in, they were not allowed to speak but it became apparent as the van drove along that the signs were now in English and that they were in the United States. They drove nonstop for the entire day until they arrived that night at a house that overlooked a river." He continued with his narrative about the escape of Soon Ling Oh from the downtown hotel., how she hid in the Kim`s restaurant and ended up in his neighbor`s basement.

Cash paused again and LaKeisha asked, "Is there more to the story?" At this point Cash described the morning`s trip into the Rust Belt cities along the Monongahela River and the discovery of the house where the other girls are being held captive.

LaKeisha pushed her chair back and said, "Wow!! Cash when you step into something you get into it up to your neck." Standing up she continued, "That was my third cup of coffee. Excuse me while I go to the ladies room. When I come back we need to figure out our next step how to rescue the girls and nail those bastards."

When LaKeisha returned from the ladies room Cash smiled and said, "I`m glad you used the word "we." All "we" have to deal with is an international drug and human trafficking cartel, Mexican air borne coyotes, an illegal immigrant in my neighbor`s basement, a drug war in the city, and don`t forget a suspected serial killer in a nursing home. This reminds me of the old joke when the Lone Ranger and Tonto come to the crest of a hill and when they looked down the hill there are two hundred Indians in war paint. When the Lone Ranger asks Tonto what should we do? Tonto looks at him and says what do you mean "we," Kemosabe?"

LaKeisha smiled and said, "Come on! Let`s go get them, Kemosabe."

CHAPTER
23

The most direct approach was the obvious, so Cash and LaKeisha drove from the Burger King directly across town to the Southside where they pulled into the parking lot at thirty three eleven East Carson Street. The unpretentious sign read Western Pennsylvania Field Office of the Federal Bureau of Investigation. The building itself was of modern design with ample use of glass and aluminum to provide a brightly lit lobby. A guard was standing at the metal detectors and after Cash and LaKeisha showed their badges, he asked them to check their revolvers. After tagging the guns, he handed each of them a receipt and directed them to the information desk.

At the information, desk they were greeted by a middle-aged lady with a name tag that read Sarah. They explained that this was an unscheduled visit but they needed to talk to an agent about an urgent matter. Sarah asked a few more questions that produced enough useful information from the detectives. She hesitatingly asked them to be seated in a waiting area and she picked up her phone. Taking seats in the aluminum and glass waiting area they were discussing how to go about contacting the United States Immigration and Customs Enforcement Agency when a slender young woman walked over and introduced herself as Agent Karen Lipke. She led them to a small generic government office with no personal pictures on the walls or desk. She sat down behind the desk and the two detectives took chairs facing her.

Sha inquired about the purpose of their visit, and also why they had considered it urgent.

Cash took the lead and gave a synopsis of the human trafficking, narcotics, and an international criminal organization operating in the Pittsburgh area. Ms. Lipke seemed dubious of the tale but after a few minutes of further discussion excused herself and left the room. Fifteen minutes later she returned with a man carrying manila folder who introduced himself as Agent Donald Graham. Before the detectives could say anything Graham said, "I`ve been looking forward to meeting you, Phillip Cash. There are a few questions I`d like you to answer."

Cash, obviously surprised by this opening statement, silently gestured with his hands for agent Graham to proceed. "Why were you in your personal vehicle doing surveillance out of your jurisdiction and who was in the car with you this morning?"

Cash recovered and asked added, "How did you get that information?"

Graham replied, "I`m the one asking the questions. What were you doing there and who was in the car with you?"

Cash answered the questions as asked.

Graham then continued, "We have had that house under observation for about ten days. We saw your car and ran the license plate." Without sitting down he said, "We all need to go up to the bureau chief`s office and share some of what we know."

On the way there, LaKeisha whispered to Cash," Yeah, like these guys like to share information."

Bobby Alberts was the newly appointed Bureau Chief of Station for the Western Pennsylvania Federal Bureau of Investigation. An African American, he had come up through the ranks and he was respected by his agents. He stood about five eleven and his athletic build carried one hundred and eighty pounds. He had played halfback in the Big Ten and his bureau history included the story of a drug dealer he had thrown through a second story window during a drug bust in Baltimore.

When they entered his office he got up from behind his desk and came over to Cash and LaKeisha. He was wearing a white shirt with his sleeves rolled up. The top button of his shirt was open and his tie was pulled down a few inches. When they shook hands Cash felt like his hand was in a vise. The handshake with LaKeisha was much more gentlemanly.

The station chief got right down to business once they were seated. "We've had the Koreans under our observation for some time now. They are out of Queens, New York, and we know that they have to move their business out of that city. They see the Rust Belt as a great opportunity. There is an opioid epidemic in this area extending from Donora here in on the Monongahela River down through Ambridge and Aliquippa along the Ohio River into West Virginia and beyond. The reason for my being posted here is to stop organized crime from turning this into their pot of gold. Your suspicions of human trafficking are the first we have heard of in this area."

Cash interrupted here and said, "These aren't suspicions. We have talked to one of the kidnaped women who escaped from the

Koreans. She was in my car and pinpointed the house where two other girls are being held."

A surprised Bobby Alberts looked at Cash and said, "What in the hell are you telling me? If I got the story right, you had an illegal alien, a victim of human trafficking by an international crime syndicate in your personal vehicle. You were totally out of your jurisdiction and trying to do the job of the Federal Bureau of Investigation."

Cash didn't blink and answered, "That's about right. That's water over the dam. Now, are we going to share information and take these guys down?"

Alberts sat back in his chair and smiled, "Well, I'll hand you this, Detective Cash, you've got balls but here is how things are going to be."

Driving back to Zone One headquarters LaKeisha began the discussion, "I don't want to say "I told you so," but so much for the sharing bit. That Bobby Alberts is the real thing. Let's review where we stand. First off, you need to take Soon Ling into custody and report her to Immigration and Custom's Enforcement. We should put a hold on her until she can be turned over to them. Secondly, you were officially told to stay in your own backyard. So now it is back to simple homicides and narcotics for us."

"Yeah, I guess you're right. Back to our boring lives. Say, I noticed you paying a lot of attention and taking a good hard look at the bureau chief. Is he your type?"

"Give me a break, Kemosabe. I'm a single mom with a full time job and a fifteen year old boy who's hormones are exploding. I don't have time for any romancing. Besides, that I'm still in love with my man, Amos, who died a hero in Viet Nam."

With that Cash realized that he had scratched open an old wound so he turned his attention to traffic as a tear rolled down LaKeisha`s cheek.

CHAPTER
24

Pak Tan Hee was dreading the phone call he needed to make to Lee Heon Tae. It was Lee who had been his mentor and introduced him to Khangpae. Lee had treated him as a little brother. Lee was there the day he got his tattoo signifying the *pa* (mob) he belonged to. Pak sat in the house overlooking Donora and the Monongahela River and let his mind wander back to when he was a teenager in Suwon, South Korea. The rice farmers were still using ox carts to take their goods to market and on one particularly frigid day as he was walking along the road he passed a pair of oxen who had icicles hanging down from their mouths as they labored along on the road to Incheon. In the summertime the sunsets were breathtaking. The silhouettes of the fishermen returning in their sampans stood in bold relief on the yellow sea. All the colors of the visible spectrum were gloriously on display. The red orange of the setting sun blended into the green, yellow, and blue of the sampan sails, while the impending night brought the indigo and violet that completed this beautiful panorama. It was as beautiful and peaceful as any place on this planet. Why did he ever leave there and how did he become involved with an international crime organization? He hated working in the stinking rice paddies with human waste as fertilizer and saw no future as the third son in his family. So he left the rice paddies and became what was considered a "slicky boy" in those days, making a few won by stealing anything he could from the U.S. Army base at Ascom City where he got a job as a house boy. The drunken soldiers were also an easy mark in the darker alleys of Bupyung.

Coming back to the reality of the task facing him, he felt embarrassed and guilty that he had let his idol down. Lowering his head in shame he dialed Lee Heon Tae`s cellphone number. On the third ring, the familiar voice of his mentor answered "Yo bo seo."

"It`s me, Heon Tae. I need to give you an update." Pak hesitated at this point and was not sure how to proceed.

"What`s going on my younger brother?" Lee asked "You sound upset."

Pak then proceeded to tell him that one of the girls in his group had escaped. That they had sold her services to a man in a hotel in downtown Pittsburgh and she somehow escaped. He told of how the three men had scoured the downtown area but found no sign of her.

Lee went ballistic over the phone *"An dwae yo!!" (It can`t be)* calling Pak every derogatory name in the Korean language. How Pak had disappointed his mentor and how he had dishonored his *pa and the only way to redeem himself was to find the girl and punish her properly.* In Khangpae, this constituted a death sentence for her. As Lee`s anger subsided, he became more pragmatic and asked Pak for more details. After getting all the information he proceeded with some advice. Obviously the girl could not have gone far in a strange city with no money and no obvious plan. Therefore, the most logical place would be the Korean restaurant.

Pak explained they had gone there and searched the entire place.

Lee exploded again, "You stupid idiot, that is where you have to go! Go back and force the owners to tell you where she is. Use whatever methods necessary but find and eliminate that girl. She knows too much!"

The chastised Pak Tan Hee (street name Tom) knew what his task was.

Kim Heon Tae sat back in his chair in the second floor office at the Korean Martial Arts School for Taekwondo and Hokkaido. He pondered what this latest development from his little brother's mission in the Rust Belt meant to the overall survival of the Incheon branch of Khangpae in America. They had been battling the Chinese Green Dragons for over twenty years for the drug and prostitution trade in Queens. At one time, they even worked with the Green Dragons to battle the mafia families for control of this turf. Once the Koreans and Chinese had control of Queens the Green Dragons turned against their oriental partners and a bloody battle began between the two sides. At first, the Khangpae held their own but eventually the overpowering numbers of Green Dragon warriors had forced the Koreans to look for other territories.

Lately, things had become more precarious when two of Kim's associates had been assassinated in a very grisly manner. There was also talk on the street that Kim himself could be the next victim. Sitting up straight in his chair he realized that he needed to go to Donora, Pennsylvania to help his little brother solidify their control in the Rust Belt. He picked up his phone and made plans accordingly.

It was closing time at the Garden of the Morning Calm restaurant, and the elder Mr. Kim was bussing the last tables and setting up for the next day's customers. He turned and walked to the front door to lock up. Looking out the front window he saw a Black Cadillac

Escalade pull up and two burly Koreans got out and came barging in, "Sorry but we are closed for dinner," he said. The larger of the two men grabbed him by his shirt and pushing him against the wall hissed "We're not here to eat, we want the girl!"

Kim immediately recognized him as the man who was there the night before, "What girl?"

Before he could say anything else, the other Korean ran back toward the kitchen as Mrs. Kim came through the door drying her hands with a towel. He grabbed her in a bear hug, turned, and carried her to where her husband was being held against the wall. Pak Tan Hee then pushed Mr. Kim to the floor knocking down several chairs. Towering over him he issued the ominous threat, if Kim wanted to see his wife alive again he would have twenty four hours to lead them to the girl's location. Kicking the fallen Mr. Kim he added, "I will call you here tomorrow morning at 8:00 A.M. and I want the answer." Then, the two thugs left carrying a struggling Mrs. Kim who they threw roughly into the back of the black Cadillac Escalade and drove off. A dazed and frightened Mr. Kim ignored the pain from being kicked in his back, got up, and rushed to the phone to call his son Henry.

CHAPTER
25

The children were upstairs in their bedrooms for the night and Laura and Phil Cash sat down in the den to relax. He had just brought in a glass of white zinfandel for her and he eased into his recliner chair with a bottle of Bud Light. Laura began to tell Phil about her day as a substitute teacher at Brian and Robin`s school. Just as Phil took his first sip of the Bud Light, the doorbell rang. "I`ll get it," he said as he slowly got up and went to the front door wondering who would be ringing their door bell at this time of night. Opening the door, he saw a frenzied Henry Kim, who blurted out "They've kidnapped my mother."

Phil motioned Henry in and they went into the den. When Laura saw Henry, she sensed something was wrong and directed him to a chair. Henry declined to sit and pacing back and forth in the den he began to tell them what had just happened at the Garden of the Morning Calm. Laura got up and put his arm on Henry`s shoulder and had him sit down in the chair. Phil sensing the emergency changed mentally from husband, father, and neighbor to his Detective Cash mode.

"Did your father call the police?"

"No, he just locked himself in the restaurant and called me."

Cash pulled out his cell phone and as he was dialing he said, "We need to get a patrol car over there right away and make sure your dad is o.k." After making the call, he turned to Henry and swore him to absolute secrecy. "I talked to the Federal Bureau of Investigation and U.S. Immigration and Customs Enforcement today. I think I know where your mother has been taken. We have scheduled a joint meeting tomorrow with the Pittsburgh Police and agents from ICE and the Federal Bureau of Investigation. These guys are good. We`ll get your mother back."

Henry holding back some tears said, "I know you will do all you can, but this looks almost hopeless."

Laura got up and going over to where Henry was sitting, she bent down and putting her arm around his shoulder said, "The police and the federal agents will do all they can, and you and I need to do what we can. We can all pray because miracles still happen."

As Laura continued to try and comfort Henry, Cash stepped into the kitchen and pulled agent Don Grahams card from his pocket and dialed the emergency number. Graham was still in the office on East Carson Street and picked up on the second ring. Cash said, "Agent Graham this is Detective Cash. We need to share again." Cash then explained the kidnapping of Mrs. Kim and the twenty-four hour deadline the kidnappers had given her husband. He added, "What these hostages need is the Federal Bureau of Investigation`s fire power."

Graham took this all in and replied, "O.K. I get the message. Here is what I can share with you. After you were here today, our bureau chief ordered me to assemble our elite Hostage Rescue Team. As we speak, they are packing up and should be in Pittsburgh by seven o`clock tomorrow morning. Can you make an early meeting? The Federal SWAT guys will want to talk with you."

"What time?"

"I've got your cell. Can you make it on half an hour's notice?"

"Absolutely!"

Walking back into the living room Cash walked over to Henry and Laura, who were reciting the Hail Mary and announced, "Keep the prayers going, we may be working on another miracle."

CHAPTER
26

December 14, 2018, 6:45 A.M.

Phil Cash had just poured a cup of coffee and was sitting down at the kitchen table with Laura when his cell phone rang. It was Agent Donald Graham.

"The Hostage Rescue Team has arrived early and they want to get a briefing started as soon as possible. How quickly can you get here? Since narcotics smuggling is also involved, Bureau Chief Alberts thought your narcotic detective might add to the meeting."

"I`ll be there as soon as I can. Traffic shouldn`t be that bad this early in the morning. Probably twenty minutes or so. I`ll call Detective Johnson and have her meet us at the bureau building."

Laura was well aware of the routine and had started some scrambled eggs and bacon. Cash went upstairs and looked in on the children, who were still sleeping. He went into the master bedroom and put on a white dress shirt and blue slacks. Picked out a conservative tie and opened the lock box holding his Glock revolver. He slid on his shoulder holster and put on a gray sport jacket and went down stairs. Before entering the kitchen, he put LaKeisha`s number on speed dial. A sleepy

Detective Johnson answered on the fourth ring and recognizing the number said, "What's the play?" Cash explained about the arrival of the Hostage Rescue Team and the request by Bobby Alberts that she attend the meeting. LaKeisha responded in the positive and added that her son has recently started walking to school, since there was a young lady in his class that he was smitten with and she lived on the way. She said she would wake him up and be on her way.

Cash then entered the kitchen and breakfast was on the table. Laura said that he had better eat before it got cold. He devoured the meal in record time. He got up took the dishes to the sink where Laura was standing and said, "Sweetie, you are the absolute best! I don't know how I could get along without you." As she hugged him she whispered into his ear, "You are the best also. I don't know how I could get along without you. I know how dangerous today could be. Please come back to me and the children tonight."

After a long lingering kiss, he turned and went out the door to the garage. She didn't realize that she still had a dish towel in her hand, so she laid it on the counter and started upstairs to get the children ready for school.

Cash arrived at the East Carson Federal Bureau of Investigation at almost twenty minutes to the second. He jogged from the parking lot up the steps into the lobby. At security, he checked his gun and was directed to a second floor auditorium. Entering the auditorium, he looked around for Detective Johnson but apparently she had not arrived yet. Standing in front of the stage was Agent Donald Graham talking animatedly to two men, and he recognized Agent Karen Lipke off to the side.

The door behind Cash opened and Bobby Alberts the station chief entered. Extending his hand he said, "Thanks for coming. How about the narcotics lady?"

"She should be along shortly. She`s a single mom and had a teenager to roust out of bed."

"Come on up front and meet some of the cavalry," Alberts said as he began to walk down the aisle to the front row.

Agent Graham stepped back as Alberts approached him and the two men Graham had been talking to. Alberts shook their hands, said a pleasantry or two, and then introduced the detective. Both men wore dark blue workmen type pants and short sleeve shirts. Cash shook hands with both men and noticed the biceps on them that would make Charles Atlas look like the weakling.

Agent Graham scrambled up on the stage and asked everyone to be seated so he could start the briefing. He electronically lowered a screen and projected the Federal Bureau of Investigation logo. Underneath the logo were the words Fidelity, Bravery and Integrity.

Just as he was about to project the next slide, Detective LaKeisha Johnson entered the back of the auditorium. Graham hesitated and said, "The detective from narcotics is here," and motioned for her to take a seat.

Of course, everyone turned to see who it was, as LaKeisha walked toward the front of the auditorium. She had on black slacks and a white turtleneck sweater both of which flattered her figure. Cash was seated in the second row on the end and moved over so she could sit next to him.

Agent Graham regained everyone`s attention, and he proceeded to the next slide. What followed was the bureau`s surveillance of the building. Heat sensors had shown three people on the first floor and two people on the second floor yesterday. This morning however it indicated a third person on the second floor.

Then Graham showed video of the traffic flow in the neighborhood. Cash sunk down in his seat a little when he saw his own car and the magnified image of his license plate. After this sequence one of the Hostage Rescue Team asked who was in that car. Graham informed the group that it was the hostage that had escaped, the husband of the latest hostage, and Detective Cash. For a few more excruciating moments, Agent Graham outlined that the detective driving the car was out of his jurisdiction and how he managed to have the illegal alien who had escaped in his car.

To Cash's great relief, Graham told of how Cash had come directly to the Bureau to share this information. At this point he discontinued the surveillance video, telling the group that it just showed them following the black Cadillac Escalade as the Korean criminals delivered the illicit drugs to the local dealers.

Then he got into illegal narcotics and emphasized how ubiquitous the drug use was in this area, and for emphasis he mentioned that it was so bad that they observed a drug drop to a dealer at a nursing home on the Northside of Pittsburgh. LaKeisha almost jumped out of her seat at this point and Cash raised his hand to get Graham's attention. Graham acknowledged him and Cash asked for him to run the video of the tail they had done on the Cadillac and to fast forward it to the nursing home. When the video got to that segment, Cash whispered to LaKeisha, "Holy shit, It's Holy Angels!" Cash said to stop the video at this point, and Graham asked what was on the video that was so important. "This is the nursing home where Detective Johnson and myself are investigating the sudden deaths of several residents from fentanyl overdosing as potential homicides." This got the attention of everyone in the auditorium. Cash and LaKeisha then answered a deluge of questions. When Graham decided to move on, he discussed smuggling drugs through the southwestern border, and the turf war for drug dealing in Pittsburgh and the rest of the Rust Belt. At this point, Cash and LaKeisha gave a summary of their ongoing investigation at Holy Angels and answered all the additional questions the federal agents asked.

As the briefing progressed, Cash volunteered that the Immigration Customs and Enforcement Agency had been notified and had placed a hold on the third hostage and that she was in protective custody. At this point, Bureau Chief Bobby Alberts got up in the front row and came over to where Cash and LaKeisha were seated and dismissed them from the rest of the meeting. He acknowledged that she was a very busy lady and thanked her for attending the meeting. As Cash was exiting the aisle, the bureau chief quietly told him that the meeting was strictly confidential and that the bureau had no intentions of sharing the surveillance video with local authorities.

CHAPTER
27

December 14, 2018, 2:48 P.M.

For the first time ever, Raymond punched in early on the time clock in the basement of Holy Angels. Changing into his blue scrubs, he rapidly made his way to the third floor and went directly to room 365. Opening the door he looked in. It was empty and appeared ready for a new patient. He stepped in and looked around the floor. It was gone! He smiled to himself. The old broad had croaked and the football player will be toast, because his wallet was found on the floor. That guy is so dumb he never locks his door!

Going down the hall to the nursing station, he reported in for work. At his meal, time he celebrated by going to Arby`s for a roast beef sandwich with extra meat rather than Taco Bell. Sitting at a table by himself, he planned his departure from Pittsburgh to places south. Someone had at one time told him that Jackson, Mississippi was a nice place.

He had already picked up his paycheck and cashed it. There was also a Christmas bonus so he could get some extra drugs from Tom this evening. His duffel bag was packed and he had skipped out of his apartment without paying this week`s rent. As soon as he got the drugs, it was off to the bus station and a Greyhound to warmer places.

December 14, 2018, 3:30 P.M.

LaKeisha looked up from her paperwork as Cash walked into the Zone One squad room. "You`re late from lunch, Kemosabe. What`s up?"

"Had to talk to Brian`s teacher again. He just isn`t with the program yet."

LaKeisha continued, "Cash, it`s genetic. Have you gotten with the mayor's program yet?"

"Of course, I have. I`m hosting a fund raiser in her honor. A thousand dollars a plate and you will be the guest speaker."

Before LaKeisha could stop laughing, Cash`s phone rang and he picked up the call.

"Holy shit, are you kidding me? Who is this guy? Fax me all the info and the mug shot."

"What was that all about?" LaKeisha asked.

"I ran the prints on that Raymond Benson guy at Holy Angels. He isn`t really Raymond Benson. He is one Raymond Boudreau and he is wanted for a double homicide in Louisiana." Getting up he grabbed his coat and said, "I`m on my way to Lockhart Street right now."

Grabbing her purse and coat LaKeisha said, "If what you say is right, this guy may be dangerous. I`m your backup, Kemosabe." After a few minutes in an unmarked car, they pulled up at five-eighteen Lockhart Street. Going in the unlocked front door, they went up the steps to the second floor and knocked on Raymond Boudreau`s door. Getting no response, Cash knocked louder. Still no response. He tried the knob and the door was unlocked. Opening the door they carefully entered. All signs of human habitation were gone and the only things present were the roaches and the empty Taco Bell bags.

"Looks like your guy rabitted on us," LaKeisha said.

Bounding down the steps he called the Holy Angels Retirement Community. When the Executive Director, Marilyn Cassidy, picked up he identified himself and asked if Raymond Benson was at work. She answered that he wasn`t due until the three to eleven shift came on. She volunteered that she knew he had come in early to pick up his paycheck, but then left the building." Cash asked her to call him immediately when Raymond Benson showed up for work. He disconnected and said to LaKeisha, "We`re heading to Taco Bell." Not finding him there they returned to the station house.

Picking up the fax and the mug shot he showed the picture to LaKeisha. She responded, "That`s our guy all right, now all we have to do is find him."

Sitting down at his desk, Cash called the sheriff`s office in New Iberia. After a ten minute talk, he hung up. Turning to LaKeisha`s desk he said, "I talked to a Deputy Sheriff, Carrie Landry. This guy has a long rap sheet for minor drug dealing and petty theft. She also thinks he vandalized her house the day before he vanished. He apparently blew away his grandmother and her live-in boyfriend with a shotgun back in August and headed north. He was last seen in Little Rock. I`ll put out a Bolo on him, but let`s hope he shows up for work."

About 4:35 P.M., Cash got a call from the Executive Director at Holy Angele that Raymond had shown up for work. LaKeisha was downstairs in the record room, so he called her on her cell. "My man just showed for work at Holy Angels. What`s the status on your drug bust with the feds tonight?"

"The Hostage Rescue Team is planning to hit the hostage house tonight. They also want to get them on a narcotics charge, so they are planning to do a double takedown at Holy Angels with our local narcotics unit and that includes me. The feds will lead the charge, but our SWAT guys will be back up. The feds will co-ordinate the timing so both raids occur simultaneously."

Cash asked "What is their time line?"

"At Holy Angels, in the parking lot at nine o`clock this evening"

"Now that we have a positive I.D. on the fentanyl killer and we know where he is, homicide needs to be in on this. Maybe we can make it a triple takedown."

LaKeisha said, "Bobby Alberts gave me his personal cell number. I`ll get in touch and see if he is willing to deal you in."

"You`re on! When do you meet with our SWAT team ?"

"In the ready room at six-thirty."

Bobby Alberts was in the gym at the East Carson Street Federal Building when he took LaKeisha`s call. He was in gym shorts and a white tee shirt, which read Doctors Without Borders, and he had just completed his daily one hundred sit ups. Wiping the perspiration from his face he answered "Yes, Detective Johnson, what can I do for you?" LaKeisha brought him up to date on the fentanyl murders and Cash`s desire to be in on the raids.

Alberts mulled this over and agreed that Cash could be present as an observer, but the federal agents would arrest the murder suspect and then turn him over to the local authorities.

CHAPTER
28

Hostage House – December 14, 2018 morning of raid

In the red brick house high on the hill overlooking the abandoned steel mill, Pak Tan Hee was conducting a strategy meeting with his Kkangpae associates. Pak nervously looked out the window at two barges loaded with coal being pushed along the Monongahela River towards the junction with the Ohio River. Standing next to him was his sponsor Lee Heon Tae. He turned slowly towards the two thugs sitting at the kitchen table eating breakfast. "We cannot fail in this mission. My mentor, Lee Heon Tae, has personally come from Queens and placed his trust in our hands. We must honor him."

Turning to Lee he bowed and asked him for any additional advice. Lee answered "It is absolutely necessary that our organization expands westward for the very survival of Kkangpae in America," Lee said to them. "My little brother, Pak Tan Hee, has outlined a plan that will insure our success and prosperity".

One of the thugs put down his fork and after wiping his mouth with a napkin said, "We are honored by your visit and understand our mission, Lee Heon Tae. We too want to bring honor and success to our organization. What is the plan?"

Pak then explained he called Mr. Kim early that morning and he was told that the girl was being hidden in a convent somewhere in West Virginia. Mr. Kim also told Pak that the girl would be returned to Pittsburgh on the premise arrangements could be made for her to return to South Korea. The girl would be in the Garden of the Morning Calm Restaurant that evening by nine o'clock. Pak continued, "I warned him not to go to the police, and if the girl was at the restaurant his wife would be returned unharmed."

"What if she isn't there?" asked one the men at the table.

"We kill both of the Kims. That will send a message to the Korean community that whoever is hiding her has to give the girl up."

"What if she is there?"

"Then we kill all three of them."

"When to we make our move?"

"You and I will leave here about seven o'clock, as usual, and make our narcotic rounds. Lee Heon Tae will accompany us. Our last stop is on the Northside with that dumb ass at the retirement home about nine o'clock. Then we turn back into downtown and finish our business at the restaurant." Pointing to the other man at the table he said, "You stay here and guard the other two girls and the old lady. We will deal with her later and remember no rough stuff with the girls. They need to look good when we start to market them in the city."

Pak seemed to relax a little now that everything seemed to be falling in place. He went over to the table and pulled out a chair and sat down, "How about one of you fixing breakfast for me and our honored guest."

Upstairs in a bedroom Mrs. Kim sat on the side of a bed and faced the two young Korean girls, who sat in separate chairs positioned on each side of a dresser. They had been up most of the night praying the rosary and other prayers, some of which were directed to Saint Jude, the patron saint of lost causes.

When she had arrived at the house, Mrs. Kim realized that the girls had no idea that they were in Pennsylvania. They had obviously been traumatized by their captors and were emotionally devastated. Despite her own plight, Mrs. Kim knew that she had to be strong for these girls and had told them that the police knew where they were being held hostage and miracles still happened. She eased herself off the side of the bed and walked to the window that was bracketed by the scalloped blue curtains. Peering out, she saw the large abandoned buildings by the river and the huge rusted Bessemer converter. She remembered a television show about the strength of the steel industry in this area during World War II and that the funny looking giant beer barrel was somehow important for making steel. Turning back toward the bed she returned to the reality at hand and said, "Korean women are strong women. We have survived the Japanese Army forcing us into sex slavery during WW II. We suffered the horrors of our country being overrun by the North Koreans and the Chinese Communist army. What we had left was a devastated third world country, but we survived and prospered. We never gave up." Taking the two girls by the hand she led them to the window and said, "God is on our side. We will survive and we will be free."

CHAPTER

29

December 14, 2019, 6:30P.M.

The testosterone was flowing as Cash entered the ready room. LaKeisha was already there. Lou Onofrio leader of the local SWAT team had just started the meeting. He acknowledged Cash and said the timeline would wait until the drug deal had been consummated. The federal agents would lead the raid and make the arrest of the murder suspect and the narcotics traffickers. The local SWAT team would be there as backup, and La Keisha would be present representing the local narcotics unit.

Cash looked around the room and even though there was enough firepower to win a minor war, he knew from having his unit ambushed in Afghanistan, that anything could go wrong at any time. When the SWAT team leader was satisfied that they were all on the same page they all loaded up and set off for Holy Angels.

The SWAT team with LaKeisha joining them took up strategic positions around the grounds of Holy Angels. Cash felt that his best location was on the first floor hall next to Warren`s apartment. It opened to the rear of the grotto and gave him a direct view to where the drug deal would go down. As he was waiting there Warren returned from a bingo game in the ballroom. Seeing Cash he asked what was going on. Cash gave him a nebulous answer and told Warren to stay in his room.

Entering his room Warren sensed something exciting was going on, so he called the rest of the Dwarfs and they assembled in Valerie`s apartment right above his to be in on the action.

At precisely eight-fifty-eight, the black Cadillac Escalade arrived and 2 minutes later Raymond exited the building and walked to the vehicle. The rear window rolled down and he handed someone what appeared to be wad of cash. Shortly thereafter, he was handed a small plastic bag and the window rolled up. Raymond turned to walk back toward the building. At this point an armored federal SWAT team vehicle drove from behind the administration building onto the parking lot and the leader of the FBI SWAT team used a bullhorn and announced in a loud voice "Raymond Boudreau, Federal Bureau of Investigation. Drop the bag and put up your hands!" Raymond stood motionless. "Drop the bag now!!" the voice on bullhorn blared. Raymond in utter fear dropped the bag. The bullhorn blurted out the next order, "Everyone in the black Cadillac step out with your hands in the air and lie down on the ground." The next instant the Cadillac began to move and accelerate toward the parking lot exit. Three federal SWAT team agents jumped out of the armored vehicle with their automatic weapons drawn and deployed themselves to the front and either side of the accelerating Cadillac. Just then the rear window of the Cadillac rolled down and the business end of an A.K.47 began to protrude out. The agent in front of the car dove out of the way and rolled over in a firing position. What followed next was a deafening roar from the armored vehicle, the remaining window and rear door of the Cadillac disappeared in a fiery ball. The Cadillac swerved out of control and crashed head on into a light stanchion in the parking lot. The armored vehicle moved quickly to block the possibility of the Cadillac backing up. The three federal agents on the ground cautiously approached the vehicle. The driver`s door and passenger doors opened and two oriental appearing men staggered out with their hands in the air and after they laid face down on the pavement were immediately handcuffed by the federal agents.

Amidst all this confusion Raymond picked up the bag of narcotics he had dropped and started running across the lawn toward the rear parking lot. Watching the events unfold from Valerie`s second story apartment, Damien saw this and rushed out of her apartment and took the stairs three at a time and out the back door to the grotto. Raymond running as fast as he could looked back to see if anyone was following him. Damien approached from the blind side and launched what was called a flying tackle in the 40s, but today is called targeting and would draw a fifteen yard penalty, a hefty fine, and expulsion from the game. Leading with his head he hit Raymond full force in the chest. All the air went out of Raymond with a giant ooooooof, and he went flying like a rag doll fifteen yards backwards. The bag of drugs flew up in the air with the pills landing like popcorn in the grass. The local SWAT team encircled the prostrate Raymond and cuffed him. Cash arrived on the scene at the same time as did one of the federal agents. After a brief discussion, it was decided that Cash would take Raymond Boudreau into custody.

A few minutes later Raymond began to regain his senses. When he saw Damien and Cash standing over him he wailed, "That son of a bitch broke some more of my ribs."

CHAPTER
30

December 14, 2018, 8:50 P.M.

The Hostage Rescue Team had assembled in a house, that had been leased by the Federal Bureau of Investigation as a surveillance post to monitor the suspected Khangpae takeover of the illegal drug trafficking in the Rust Belt. The house was in a residential area about a quarter of a mile up the hill from the house, which was now being referred to as the hostage house. A final briefing was underway and new observations revealed another Korean male had arrived late the prior evening in a rented Kia van. Jim Donaldson was the leader of the team and local agent Don Graham was going along during the raid.

The local section head, Bobby Alberts, much to his disappointment was remaining back in the surveillance house. He realized he was no longer an active field agent in the middle of the action, but was now just an observer and on the bench.

The cool professionalism of the team prevailed as the agents put on their Kevlar vests and helmets. Weapons were checked and rechecked.

Donaldson emphasized the precise timing, as the two planned raids depended on surprising the Koreans at exactly the same time. He then gave the radio frequency to the station chief Alberts so he could monitor the action in real time.

When all was ready the six man team left and took up their planned positions. One man was stationed across the street from the front door. Two were stationed on the right of the building covering the garage. The other three were to enter through the kitchen in the back. There was no exit from the left side of the building.

The first radio transmission came twenty minutes later. Donaldson`s voice simply said that the Cadillac had left the premises with two men in the front seat and one man in in the rear seat. The man in the rear seat appeared to have an automatic weapon.

The team deployed at Holy Angels confirmed they had received the message

The radio remained silent until eight fifty eight when the team leader at Holy Angels reported, "All units go!" and both teams went into action simultaneously.

The back door of the hostage house was kicked in and the three SWAT team agents burst into the kitchen. They already knew the location of all the inhabitants of the building from heat sensor technology, which had been used in their planning. The three people upstairs were the three women hostages and one person on the first floor in the living room. After the agents entered the kitchen they deployed two "flash bangs" into the living room and quickly ducked back outside. The Korean guarding the hostages was totally taken by surprise, as he had been relaxing watching reruns of the TV show M*A*S*H.

The three SWAT team members rushed back in through the kitchen and into the living room. The guard was still temporarily blinded and deafened from the "flash bangs" and was easily subdued and cuffed with zip ties. When the agents were satisfied that all the guard's weapons were accounted for, one of the agents went upstairs to the bed room where the hostages were being held. On opening the door he saw the two young girls cowering behind the bed. The seventy- two year old Mrs. Kim was standing between the Hostage Rescue Team agent and the two girls. She was holding a table lamp by its shaft brandishing the base as a weapon. Mrs. Kim realized what was happening and dropped the lamp and ran to the agent and hugged him through his Kevlar vest whispering, "Our prayers have been answered." He lowered his automatic rifle only after he was sure the room was secured.

Bobby Alberts had been watching the hostage house with binoculars and had seen the flash through the living room windows. What seemed like an eternity to him, but was only a few minutes, until radio contact was made and team leader Donaldson reported that the suspect was in custody and all three of the hostages were safe.

EPILOGUE

December 15, 2018

Lieutenant Sam Kalina came bouncing into the squad room at eight-ten A.M. brandishing a copy of the Pittsburgh Press. " Have you guys seen the headlines in the morning paper?" Spreading it out on LaKeisha`s desk, the headlines read "Former Steeler Linebacker Tackles Serial Killer." Beneath it in bold print it read, "Mayor praises police for outstanding work identifying the murderer."

On the front page picture, they recognized a younger Damien standing next to a player identified as Bullet Bill Dudley. Lieutenant Kalina asked, "Who is this other guy?

LaKeisha said, "I never heard of him."

Cash stood up and said, "Let me educate both of you. I checked him out on the internet. Bullet Bill Dudley was one of the greatest players of his era. He is in the National Football League Hall of Fame. One season back in the forties he led the league in rushing, punt returns and interceptions. He would play all 60 minutes and never came off the field. Yesterday in my mind, Damien Skrcyzinski proved that he is just as big a hero as Bullet Bill."

December 20, 2018, 7:00P.M.

Laura and Phil Cash were walking along Sixth Street toward the Garden of the Morning Calm Restaurant. Pittsburgh's Golden Triangle was aglitter with the holiday decorations and Santa and his elves were busy in the department store window loading his sleigh. As they stopped to check it out, Phil confessed he hadn't bought Laura's Christmas present yet. She squeezed his hand and said, "Since you've been so busy recently, I went ahead and bought a lovely gold necklace that has a pendant with the image of the Blessed Virgin holding the Christ Child. You really have good taste, Detective Cash."

"In jewelry and women!" He replied as they continued to the restaurant.

When they entered, it was apparent that this was a good night for business as most of the tables were occupied. Henry Kim came up to greet them and escorted them to a private room off to one side. "Dad is back in the kitchen with my mother and my wife, Hilda, helping with the orders. I'm moonlighting as host. How about something to drink?"

Laura ordered a glass of white zinfandel and Cash asked for an Asahi beer. Before their drinks arrived, Henry had returned to the front door and escorted the rest of the guests to the dining area. The group included Agent Donald Graham and his wife, the six members of the Pittsburgh SWAT team, and coming in a few minutes later was a glowing LaKeisha Johnson, who was escorted by the Federal Bureau of Investigation station chief Bobby Alberts. Henry and his wife, Hilda, joined the group. After a few minutes of socializing, the elder Mr. Kim and his wife came in and asked everyone to be seated. The Kim's thanked everyone in attendance and especially thanked Bobby Alberts for the federal agents, who had lived up to their motto of Fidelity, Bravery, and Integrity.

Mr. Kim then announced that they would be served a traditional Korean meal featuring kimchi, bolgogi, and a rice dish with a secret sauce known only to Mrs. Kim.

As the dinner conversation evolved, Bobby Alberts reported that Immigration, Customs and Enforcement Agency had informed him that Soon Ling Oh and the two other girl hostages had applied for asylum and would be in protective custody until their cases would be heard.

As the dinner party wound down, Laura and Phil Cash were the first to leave citing the need to get home early because their babysitter had school the next day. On the drive back to Fineview, Laura mentioned that she was sitting next to LaKeisha and emphasized that she wasn`t eavesdropping, but had heard LaKeisha tell Bobby Alberts how difficult it was to raise a teen age boy as a single mom. Laura said that Bobby Alberts said he would be happy to talk to LaKeisha`s son, if LaKeisha wanted him to. Cash kept his eyes on the road and chuckled, "That sure was a lot to accidentally hear."

Laura softly punched him on the shoulder and said, "Never you mind how acute my hearing is. Just keep your eyes on the road."

December 22, 2018

The bulletin board at Holy Angels Retirement Community showed today`s outing as a trip to the mall and lunch on your own. At breakfast, Damien and the Dwarfs agreed that it looked like a fun outing. So at ten thirty, they met in the lobby and waited for the bus to arrive. It was a rare sunny and bright day for December in Pittsburgh and the mood in the lobby with the other residents was festive.

When the bus arrived they all boarded and off they went to the mall.

Traveling out McKnight Road, they arrived at their destination. The more agile of the residents got off first and then the walkers were taken down and opened on the pavement. Valerie claimed hers and the group entered the main entrance of the mall.

'What do we you want to do?" Millie asked the group. Valerie was quick to respond "Let`s go to the food court, I`m hungry."

Warren countered with, "You`re always hungry. I want to go to J.C. Pennys and look for a Christmas gift for my sister."

Rita suggested Chicos because she had seen an ad in the paper about a pre -Christmas sale. Millie thought that was a good idea, and Damien said he would walk along with them and do some window shopping.

Warren grumbled that he would go with Valerie to keep her company. So the group broke up. Warren complaining he was not really hungry, as he and Valerie arrived at the elevator to go to the food court on the second level.

Millie and Rita found Chicos and saw a lovely blouse on sale for forty per cent off. Damien continued on walking through the mall.

Twenty minutes later when Millie and Rita were convinced Chicos did not have their size they left the store and headed for the center of the mall, where three halls radiated off a central fountain. As they looked at the fountain, they stopped and saw Damien surrounded by a small group of teenage girls. One of the girls had just handed Damien a book and opened it up and was showing him something on one of the pages. The girl then handed him a pen and Damien wrote something in the book and gave it back to her. As Rita and Millie drew closer to the group, the young girl turned to one of her friends and excitedly said, "This is the guy that caught the serial killer! His picture was in the paper and I recognized him. He's also a famous football player. I just bought this book about the Steelers for my dad's Christmas present and this guy's picture is in it and he autographed it for me."

Either the teenage girls or Damien's towering over them caught the attention of three teenage boys, so they came over and joined the group, "Did you really play for the Steelers?" one of the boys asked.

Damien smiled and said, "Yes I did, and Bill Dudley was my friend and teammate."

"Bill who?"

Other questions came in rapid fire. Did he play with Terry Bradshaw? How many Super Bowl rings did he have? Damien seemed to be in his glory and answered all the questions politely. A few of the other girls asked Damien for his autograph.

Other shoppers passing by noticed the small crowd and Rita could see that some of them also recognized Damien.

Damien looked over and saw Millie and Rita and he said to the girl with the book, "I hope your dad likes his Christmas present." Pointing to Millie and Rita he said, "My friends are here so I better go." The three of them left and took the elevator to the second level and headed for the food court. After lunch, they returned to the bus and all the residents, except Warren and Valerie were already on board. At the last minute Valerie and Warren came hurrying out of the mall. Valerie going as fast as she could with her walker.

When they had settled down Millie and Rita described the episode of Damien and the teenagers. Warren patted Damien on the shoulder and said, "That's really great. That's something you will always remember."

Damien replied, "I'll try to remember but I may not. The important thing is that those young people will remember me."